MYTHS AND MAGIC

A SPELLBOUND BOOKSHOP PARANORMAL COZY MYSTERY

BOOK 3

J. A. WHITING

Copyright 2024 J.A. Whiting and Whitemark Publishing

Cover copyright 2024 Signifer Book Design

Formatting by Signifer Book Design

Proofreading by Donna Rich (donnarich@me.com) and Riann Kohrs (www.riannkohrs.com)

This book is a work of fiction. Names, characters, places, or incidents are products of the author's imagination or are used fictitiously. Any resemblance to locales, actual events, or persons, living or dead, is entirely coincidental.

All rights reserved.

No part of this publication can be reproduced or transmitted in any form or by any means, electronic or mechanical, without permission in writing from J. A. Whiting.

To hear about new books and book sales, please sign up for my mailing list at:
jawhiting.com

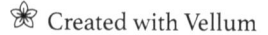

❀ Created with Vellum

Use your magic for good

1

Sitting at her small kitchen table in her cozy apartment above the Spellbound Bookshop, Shelby Price scrolled through the morning news on her phone while taking sips of her steaming coffee. Harper, her faithful feline companion, perched on the chair beside her, watching the young woman with curious eyes.

Looking up from her phone, Shelby confided to Harper, "I've had this knot in my stomach since I woke up this morning, like something isn't quite right." She set her phone down with a sigh and rubbed her temples.

Shelby's thoughts drifted to the previous Christmas when she had fallen from a ladder while decorating the bookshop. When she regained consciousness, she discovered she had an extraordinary ability - she could hear Harper's words in her mind. Since then, she had begun to experience intuitive hunches, premonitions, and paranormal sensations that, at times, unsettled her.

Harper flicked her tail. "You're probably just worried about the big sale today. Don't stress so much."

"I don't think that's it," Shelby mused, glancing at the time. "We'd better head downstairs and finish getting the shop ready. We open in twenty minutes." She quickly loaded her breakfast dishes into the dishwasher and made her way down the wooden staircase with Harper following close behind.

"Are you sure you don't sense anything unusual?" Shelby paused on the steps and nervously pushed her long brown hair over her shoulder.

Harper padded past her. "Time will tell. For now, let's just focus on the sale."

The Spellbound Bookshop was a charming haven for book lovers and curiosity seekers. Tall shelves lined the walls with a diverse collection of novels, histories, cookbooks, children's stories, and non-fiction books. Antique furniture, plush armchairs, a fireplace, and colorful displays created

Myths and Magic

a warm, inviting atmosphere that encouraged visitors to linger and explore.

Spellbound Books had a perfect location on Hamlet's pretty Main Street next to other local businesses like the Bread and Roses Bakery, The Quilted Heart Fabric Shop, and Maggie's Candle Company. Shelby had always wanted to own her own bookstore. After graduating from Boston University with a degree in literature and business, she had saved every penny she made, and two years ago, she opened her cozy shop.

Shelby also hosted author events and book clubs, and Spellbound Books now had a loyal customer base in addition to a steady stream of tourists attracted by the town's old-fashioned charm.

Hamlet was founded in the late 1600s by Puritan settlers seeking religious freedom and fertile farmland. The town sat near the rocky New England coastline not far from the better-known tourist destination of Salem. Hamlet had a rich history of spooky legends about ghosts, witches, and unexplained occurrences dating back centuries. The tales added to the area's mystique and appeal to sightseers.

Shelby busied herself with the opening tasks, making last-minute changes to the eye-catching merchandise displays and restocking a few shelves.

She retrieved the cash from the safe and carefully counted it before placing it in the register. As her employees arrived, they exchanged friendly greetings and casual conversation.

Rachel, a bright-eyed young woman, gushed about her blossoming romance with her boyfriend, Chad, a barista at a nearby coffee shop. "Things are going so well between us. He's such a sweetheart."

Patrice, a stylish older woman, chimed in, "That's wonderful, Rachel. I'm glad to hear things are going well for you and Chad." She carried paper bags to the cashier's station and placed them on the shelf under the counter. "Ron and I are planning a day trip to Boston this weekend. It'll be nice to get away for a bit."

When the clock struck opening time, a line of eager customers had already formed outside the door. Tourists and locals streamed into the shop, drawn by the promise of incredible deals and literary treasures. The store hummed with excited chatter and the rustle of turning pages.

"Shelby," a man's voice called out, and she turned to see her dear friend James Peacock. She greeted the man with a warm hug.

Mr. Peacock was a retired lawyer who now worked part-time at the library. He was also an author of crime fiction novels and articles and books on the history of Massachusetts.

"It's nice to see you," she told him. "It's going to be a crazy day."

"I love sale days," Mr. Peacock told her with a smile as he juggled several books in his arms. In his seventies, the man had lost his wife not long ago. "We must get together soon for coffee or lunch."

"I'd love to. Will you text me?"

"You know I will." Mr. Peacock wandered off to find more books he'd been hoping to read. "See you soon."

As Shelby wove through the crowd, a peculiar book caught her eye. Resting on a display table, a small, aged leather-bound volume seemed out of place among the newer releases. Intrigued, she approached the table for a closer look. Strange symbols and words in an unfamiliar language adorned the cover, and when she reached out to touch it, a tingling sensation danced across her fingertips like tiny electric sparks.

Harper leapt onto the table, her green eyes fixed on the mysterious book.

"Look at this," Shelby whispered. "I've never seen this book before. Where did it come from?"

The cat tilted her head, and her fur stood on end

as she scrutinized the worn leather binding. "Maybe a customer brought it in yesterday, put it down while browsing, and forgot it here." Harper looked at the young woman. "Or maybe someone left it for you."

Shelby frowned. "Why would someone do that?" She carefully opened the cover, revealing pages filled with indecipherable text. "I can't read it. Do you recognize this language?"

"I don't." Harper's tail swished thoughtfully. "Why don't you put it in your office for now? Keep it safe until we can figure out what it is."

"Why do I need to keep it safe?" Shelby asked, a hint of unease creeping into her voice.

"It wasn't here before," Harper pointed out. "It could be a gift, or it could be something else entirely, but we don't have time to investigate right now. Better to err on the side of caution."

A shiver ran down Shelby's spine as she gingerly picked up the book, holding it as if it might suddenly come alive and devour her. She hurried to her office and placed the puzzling volume in the drawer of her file cabinet, brushing her hands off on her jeans to try to push away the unsettling energy and sense of foreboding that clung to her like cobwebs.

With a deep breath, Shelby returned to the bustling

sales floor, determined to focus on her customers and push the strange book from her mind ... for now. This was supposed to be a festive day for the bookshop, and she wouldn't let a mysterious book ruin it.

Although she tried to focus on helping the customers, her thoughts kept drifting back to the strange book now sitting in her office. What was it? Where did it come from? Why did it make her skin tingle when she touched it?

While rearranging a display of new releases, she felt Harper rub against her leg. "You're distracted," the cat's voice echoed in her mind.

"I can't stop thinking about that book," Shelby admitted. "What if it's dangerous? Should we get rid of it?"

Harper considered this. "Let's not be hasty. Until the sale is over, keep it locked away and out of your mind."

Shelby nodded, realizing Harper was right. There were too many unanswered questions. She couldn't simply discard the book without learning more about it first.

A customer waved Shelby over, interrupting her thoughts. She plastered on a smile and went to help, pushing her concerns aside for the time being. The sale was in full swing and there were patrons to assist.

But despite her best efforts, Shelby's eyes kept drifting to the office where the mysterious book waited. She had an uneasy feeling there was more to its sudden appearance than she realized. Only time would tell what secrets the old book held.

As she helped the customer find the new releases section, Shelby heard a noise and looked out the front window. For a moment, she thought she saw a shadowy figure standing outside, watching her. She blinked and looked again, but there was no one there.

You're getting paranoid, she scolded herself. But the prickly feeling on the back of her neck felt like unseen eyes following her every move.

As she rang up a stack of paperbacks for a woman, Shelby noticed a man lingering near the display of antique books. He wore a long black coat and kept glancing around before returning his attention to the books. He had a wide nose, high cheekbones, and piercing brown eyes.

Shelby's senses tingled. Something about him set her on edge. She watched closely as he selected a large, ornate book and tucked it under his arm. He started edging toward the exit.

Making an excuse to her customer, Shelby hurried over. "Excuse me, sir. I'd be happy to ring that up for you."

The man turned sharply, clutching the book. His eyes narrowed. "I don't think so," he hissed through clenched teeth. Shelby detected a slight accent. Russian, perhaps.

She stood firm. "Then I'll hold it for you at the counter while you make up your mind."

For a moment, she thought he might flee, but after a tense pause, he reluctantly handed over the book. Shelby noted it was a rare first edition, worth quite a lot.

"My apologies," the man muttered, turning to leave. With her pulse racing, Shelby watched him exit.

Harper padded over to where she stood holding the expensive book. "I don't like the looks of that fellow," the cat remarked. "He seemed ready to fight you for this."

Shelby just nodded and after helping the customer she was waiting on, she noticed her best friend Lucy enter the shop.

Twenty-seven-year-old Lucy Blake had blue eyes, chin-length blonde hair, and a warm, friendly, optimistic attitude. She worked as a pastry chef at the fancy bed and breakfast near the town common in the center of Hamlet.

"Who was that guy?" Lucy asked, looking over her shoulder. "He bumped into me hard when he was leaving the bookshop and didn't even apologize."

"It seems he was trying to steal one of our antique books," Shelby explained.

"Really? What a loser." Lucy turned her eyes to the hustle and bustle of the shop. "Wow, it's really hopping in here. The sale must be going very well."

Suddenly, she noticed the concerned look on Shelby's face. "Don't let that guy bother you. There are lots of people with sticky fingers who try to steal whatever they can get their hands on. Forget him. You caught him, and he's gone now."

"It's not just him." Shelby sighed. "The day has gotten off to a very strange start. Come to the office, and I'll tell you all about it."

2

As the Spellbound Bookshop's sale continued in full swing, Shelby and Harper led Lucy to the backroom office. Shelby carefully lifted the mysterious leather-bound book from her file cabinet drawer. She approached Lucy, who was admiring a display of colorful bookmarks set on Shelby's desk.

Shelby kept her voice low. "This is what I wanted you to see. I found it this morning on one of the display tables. I've never seen it before, and I don't know where it came from."

Lucy's blue eyes widened with curiosity. "Ooh, let's take a look."

Shelby carried the book to a small, round table so they could examine it in the privacy of her office. After placing the tome on the table, she carefully opened the cover, revealing the peculiar symbols and foreign text inside.

Lucy leaned in for a closer look with her eyes narrowed in concentration. "Wow, this is really old. And those symbols ... I've never seen anything like them before. What language do you think this is?"

Shelby shook her head. "I have no idea. I've never come across something like this."

Harper jumped up onto the table, her green eyes fixed on the book. "It feels like there's some kind of energy coming from it," the cat remarked, her tail swishing back and forth. "I can't quite put my paw on it, but there's something special about this book."

Lucy looked at Shelby quizzically. "What's Harper saying?"

Shelby smiled, remembering that Lucy couldn't hear Harper's thoughts as she could. "She says the book feels like it has some kind of energy. I feel it too, like a tingling sensation when I touch it. It's almost as if the book is alive, somehow. It kind of gives me the creeps."

Shelby reached for the rose quartz crystal pendant that she always wore. It had been given to her by her mother and grandmother. The rose quartz was known to be a protective, healing crystal and a stone of unconditional love that inspired compassion and promoted friendship, deep healing, and peace.

Lucy reached out and gently ran her fingers over the aged leather cover of the book. "You know what? I can almost feel it, too. It's like there's a very subtle pulse beneath the surface. This is clearly no ordinary book. We need to find out what it is and where it came from."

Just then, the bell above the shop's door buzzed, and a tall, elegant woman in her mid-forties entered. She had long, dark hair pulled back in a sleek ponytail and wore a tailored black suit that lent an air of sophistication. The woman's sharp, intelligent eyes scanned the shop, looking past all the customers before landing on Shelby and Lucy coming into the room from the office.

The woman approached them with a polite smile. "Excuse me, I was hoping you might be able to help me. You're the owner of the bookstore, aren't you?" she said, looking at Shelby. "I'm looking for a very old book. It is quite rare and unusual. It's bound in aged leather and contains symbols and text in an ancient language."

Shelby and Lucy exchanged a quick glance, realizing the woman's description sounded eerily similar to the book they had just been examining.

Shelby cleared her throat, trying to maintain a casual demeanor. "We do have a wide variety of antique and rare books. Can you tell me more about the specific book you're looking for?"

The woman's piercing gaze seemed to bore into Shelby's brown eyes. "It's a very special book, one that I believe may have significant historical and … shall we say, mystical value. I've been searching for it for quite some time. A colleague told me I should look here for it."

Harper's fur stood on end, and she let out a low growl. "I don't trust her," the cat warned Shelby with her mind. "She seems too interested in the book. We need to be careful. Don't tell her much."

Shelby subtly nodded to Harper before turning back to the woman. "You know, I think we might have a book that fits that description, but we keep our most valuable and delicate books off-site for safekeeping. If you'd like, I can check our inventory and see if we have it available."

The woman's eyes narrowed slightly, but she maintained her composure. "I see. Well, as a historian, I would be most grateful if you could allow me to examine the book more closely. I assure you, I would handle it with the utmost care."

Shelby hesitated, thinking about the mysterious

volume she'd left on the table in her office. She knew she couldn't let the woman see it, not until she had a chance to learn more about its secrets herself.

"I apologize, but our off-site inventory isn't available for public viewing," Shelby explained, hoping her lie sounded convincing. "If you're interested in purchasing the book, I can certainly look into it and let you know if we still have it in stock. I'll have to go to the physical location to be certain."

The woman's lips pressed into a thin line, and for a moment, Shelby thought she might argue, but then, the woman's expression softened, and she gave a curt nod.

"Very well. If you do happen to locate the book, I would be willing to pay a substantial sum for it. Here is my card." She produced a sleek, black business card with gold letters from her purse and handed it to Shelby. "Please do keep me informed."

"I will. I'll let you know."

With that, the woman turned and strode out of the shop, her high heels clicking on the hardwood floor.

Lucy let out a breath she hadn't realized she'd been holding. "Okay, that was intense. Who do you think she is? And why is she so interested in that book?"

Shelby stared down at the business card in her hand. It read: "Evelyn Blackwell, Antiquarian and Historical Consultant." There was a phone number and email address listed below.

"I have no idea," Shelby admitted, "but I have a very strong feeling there's more to this book than meets the eye. We need to find out what it is and why someone like her would be so eager to get her hands on it."

Harper nodded in agreement. "We should be careful, Shelby. If that woman is as determined as she seems, she might not take no for an answer. We need to keep the book safe and try to uncover its secrets ourselves."

Shelby tucked the business card into her pocket. "You're right," she told the cat. "We'll have to be cautious. There's a reason this book found its way to us, and we need to discover what it is. I'll keep it in the safe just in case someone decides to visit the store when it's closed."

Lucy's eyes sparkled with excitement. "This is way more interesting than just another day baking in the inn's kitchen. This is really cool. An old book winds up in your bookshop and you have no idea how it got here, then an hour later, someone comes looking for it. What a great mystery. We'll all figure it out together, just like the Scooby Gang."

Shelby couldn't help but laugh at her friend's enthusiasm. "Okay, Scooby Gang it is, but first, I need to get back to the sale. I can't let this distract me from our customers."

After Shelby and Lucy left the sales floor for the office, Shelby carefully locked the small, mysterious book in her safe, feeling something big was about to begin. The appearances of the strange volume and the enigmatic Evelyn Blackwell seemed far more than just coincidence.

"I wonder if there's anyone in town who might be able to help us learn more about the book," Lucy mused as they went back out to the main floor of the shop. "Maybe someone at the university or the historical society?"

Shelby considered the idea. "That's a good thought. I know Professor Jeffrey Rundle at the university is an expert in medieval texts. He might be able to shed some light on the language and symbols in the book."

Harper's ears perked up. "And don't forget about Fiona Medley and Magill Binney. Both are powerful psychics. If anyone can sense and understand the energy coming from the book, it would be them."

Fiona was an intuit who owned the Crow's Crossing boutique a few blocks from the bookshop. The woman had helped Shelby better understand and improve her skills. A longtime Hamlet resident, Magill Binney was in her late seventies and was a loved and respected psychic with amazing powers.

Shelby nodded, feeling a spark of hope. "You're right, Harper. We have some excellent resources here in town, and I think we're going to need them. Let's see what we can find out."

As they rejoined the bustling activity of the sale, Shelby's mind raced with possibilities. The mysterious book had appeared in her shop for a reason, and she was determined to uncover its secrets. With the help of her friends and the unique talents of Hamlet's residents, she hoped they could piece together why it had shown up and what they should do with it.

Little did they know that the arrival of the ancient book would set in motion a chain of events that would test their courage, their friendships, and their understanding of the world around them. The secrets and magic contained within its pages held great power and would lead Shelby and her friends on a journey beyond anything they could have imagined.

3

At 8 pm the last customer left the Spellbound Bookshop, and Shelby let out a sigh of relief. The book sale had been a resounding success, with hundreds of satisfied customers and a significant boost in revenue. With a warm smile, she turned to her employees, Rachel, Patrice, and the others.

"Thank you all so much for your hard work today," Shelby said, her voice filled with gratitude. "I sure couldn't have done it without you."

Rachel grinned, her eyes sparkling with enthusiasm. "It was a blast, Shelby. The customers were so excited about the sale, and it felt great to help them find the perfect books."

Patrice nodded in agreement, her silver-gray hair gleaming under the shop's warm lighting. "It was a wonderful day, indeed, but you look exhausted, dear. Why don't you head upstairs and get some rest?"

Shelby hesitated, her eyes looking toward the back office where the mysterious book lay hidden. "I will after I finish up the closing tasks. It won't take long. I have some things to take care of upstairs, so I'll be finishing up for the day soon. Why don't you all head out? It's been a long day."

With a final round of thanks and goodbyes, the employees left, and thirty minutes later, Shelby locked up the shop and made her way to the back office. She retrieved the ancient book from its hiding place in the safe, and carefully cradled it in her arms as she climbed the stairs to her cozy apartment above the bookshop with Harper leading the way.

As she entered her apartment, the smell of the lasagna she had prepared that morning in her slow cooker filled the air, making her stomach grumble.

"Your dinner smells delicious," Harper purred, rubbing against Shelby's legs. "But I can sense your unease. The book is weighing on your mind, isn't it?"

Shelby nodded, setting the book down on her coffee table. "I can't stop thinking about it. There's something about this book that feels ... important. Like it holds the key to a great mystery."

As she dished out the lasagna for herself and

filled Harper's bowl with her favorite cat food, her eyes kept wandering to the ancient book. Its weathered leather cover seemed to beckon her, urging her to uncover its secrets.

After dinner, Shelby and Harper settled onto the couch, the book resting between them. Shelby's fingers trembled slightly as she reached out and opened the cover, revealing the first page of cryptic text.

"I can't make any sense of these symbols," Shelby murmured, her brow furrowed in concentration. "It's like no language I've ever seen."

Suddenly, as if responding to her words, the strange characters on the page began to swim and dance before her eyes. Shelby blinked, wondering if her mind was playing tricks on her, but as she watched in astonishment, the symbols seemed to rearrange themselves, morphing into familiar letters and words.

"Oh, my gosh. Look at that," Shelby cried, her voice filled with wonder. "The words have changed into English. I can read them now."

Harper leaned in closer, her eyes widening. "So can I. It's like the book is translating itself for us."

Together, Shelby and the cat began to read the first section, their eyes eagerly devouring the now-understandable text. The book spoke of a powerful artifact hidden somewhere within the town of Hamlet, an object of great magical significance that had been sought after for centuries.

The section delved into the history of the artifact, hinting at its incredible power and the dire consequences that could befall the world if it fell into the wrong hands. However, the nature of the artifact itself remained a mystery, its true identity cloaked in riddles and obscure references. They had no idea what the artifact could be.

As they read on, Shelby and Harper learned of a guardian, chosen by fate to protect both the book and the artifact. The guardian's role was to ensure the artifact remained hidden and safe, away from those who would seek to use its power for evil purposes.

Shelby's heart raced as she reached the final line of the section, the words seeming to leap off the page and into her soul. "The person who possesses this book is its guardian," she whispered aloud, her voice trembling with a mixture of excitement and fear.

Harper looked up at the young woman, her eyes wide with realization. "That means you, Shelby. You're the guardian."

Shelby felt the blood drain from her face as the

weight of the revelation settled over her. She stood up and began to pace the room, her mind reeling with the implications of what they had just learned.

"Me? The guardian of some ancient, magical artifact?" Shelby shook her head in disbelief. "This sounds like a fantasy adventure story. How is that even possible, Harper? I'm just an ordinary person, a bookshop owner. I don't have any great, special powers – certainly not strong enough powers to fight off anyone who wants this book so badly."

Harper jumped down from the couch and wound herself around Shelby's legs, offering comfort and support. "But you do. Your intuition, your premonitions, your connection with the supernatural ... those are your powers. The book chose you for a reason."

Shelby sank back down onto the couch, her fingers absently tracing the worn leather cover of the book. "But what am I supposed to do now? How do I protect an artifact when I don't even know what it is or where to find it?"

"We'll figure it out together," Harper assured her, nuzzling Shelby's hand. "We have the book to guide us, and we have each other. We'll unravel this mystery one step at a time."

Shelby nodded, taking a deep breath to steady

herself. She knew that Harper was right. The book had come into her possession for a reason, and she couldn't ignore the responsibility that had been thrust on her ... although she wished she could.

As the evening wore on, Shelby and Harper reread section one of the ancient tome, searching for clues and trying to decipher the cryptic messages hidden within its pages. The more they read, the more convinced Shelby became that the artifact was somewhere nearby, waiting to be discovered and protected.

With each passing minute, she felt a growing sense of determination, and as the clock struck 10 pm, she closed the book and hugged it to her chest before placing it on the coffee table. She looked down at her cat, a fierce resolve burning in her eyes.

"We're going to find that artifact," she declared, her voice filled with conviction. "And we're going to protect it, no matter what."

Harper purred in agreement, her tail swishing with anticipation. Together, the guardian and her feline companion were about to start on a journey that would test their courage, their wits, and their belief in the impossible. The magic of Hamlet was counting on them, and they were ready to embrace it, one page at a time.

Myths and Magic

∽

As Shelby and Harper sat on the sofa together, a sudden knock at the door startled them. Shelby's heart raced as she glanced at the small, ancient book lying open on the coffee table, its secrets exposed for anyone to see.

"Quick, Harper," Shelby whispered urgently. "We need to hide the book before anyone sees it."

The cat nodded in understanding, and together they scurried around the apartment, searching for the perfect hiding spot. Shelby carefully closed the book and slid it beneath a stack of magazines on her bookshelf, hoping it would blend in with her eclectic collection.

With the book safely concealed, Shelby took a deep breath and made her way to the door. "Who is it?" she called out, trying to keep her voice steady.

"It's me, Travis," a familiar voice replied from the other side of the door.

A wave of relief washed over Shelby as she swung the door open, revealing the handsome Detective Travis Whitely standing on her second-floor porch. His warm smile and friendly demeanor instantly put her at ease, and she couldn't help but return his grin.

Thirty-year-old Travis was tall and fit with broad shoulders, dark brown eyes, and brown hair. He was an experienced and well-respected detective, and Shelby had recently helped him solve two crimes that had been committed in the area.

Harper hurried to greet the young man, rubbing against his legs and purring contentedly. The detective chuckled and reached down to scratch the cat behind her ears. "Hey there, Harper. Always good to see you."

Travis and Shelby had become close friends over the past several months, ever since she'd helped him with the two perplexing cases. Their friendship had blossomed, and they both admitted to feeling a mutual attraction. However, they'd decided to take things slowly, building a strong foundation of friendship before rushing into a romantic relationship.

As Travis stepped into the apartment, his sharp detective instincts immediately picked up on Shelby's slightly rattled manner. "Is everything okay? You look a little shaken up."

Shelby hesitated for a moment, unsure of how much to reveal, but as she looked into Travis's kind, concerned eyes, she knew she could trust him with the truth. He was aware of her unusual skills, and having grown up in Salem, Massachusetts, he was accepting of paranormal abilities and possibilities.

"Actually, something strange happened at the bookshop today," Shelby began, leading Travis over to the couch. "I found an old book placed on one of the display tables. I'd never seen it before. Then about two hours later, a mysterious woman came in looking for it."

Travis raised an eyebrow, intrigued. "An old book? What was so special about it?"

Shelby took a deep breath and continued. "The book is written in a language I've never seen before, but somehow, when I opened it, the words started to change. They became readable like the book was translating itself into English for me."

With wide eyes, Travis leaned forward, his interest piqued. "What did you discover from reading it?"

"The book mentioned an artifact hidden somewhere in Hamlet," Shelby explained, her words spoken with a serious tone. "It's something powerful and important, and the book says it must be protected at all costs. And apparently, now I'm supposed to be the guardian of both the book and the artifact."

Travis's mouth dropped open in surprise. "You?

The guardian? How do you know it's referring to you specifically?"

Shelby shook her head, still trying to wrap her mind around the revelation. "The book said that whoever possesses it is the chosen guardian, and since it found its way to me, I guess that means I'm the one responsible for keeping it safe."

Travis nodded slowly, processing the information. "And what about the woman who came into the shop looking for it?"

Shelby explained their interaction and showed him the business card she left.

Travis held the card in his hand. "I don't recognize the name. Maybe she's from out of town." Handing the card back to Shelby, he asked, "So, what's your plan? How are you going to find this artifact and protect it?"

Shelby stood up and began pacing the room, her mind racing. "I don't know exactly, but I know I have to find it first. Once I have it in my possession, we can figure out how to keep it safe from anyone who might want to use its power for the wrong reasons."

Travis rose from the couch and placed a comforting hand on Shelby's shoulder. "You don't have to do this alone. I'll help you any way I can, and I'm sure Lucy will want to help, too. Fiona has always given you good advice over the past few months. You can count on her as well."

Shelby felt a surge of gratitude for the detective. His support and willingness to stand by her side meant more than she could express. "Thank you, Travis. I don't know what I'd do without you."

Travis smiled softly, his eyes locking with hers. "That's what friends are for, right? And who knows, maybe this adventure will lead us somewhere new."

Shelby blushed slightly, her heart fluttering against her ribs. "Maybe it will," she agreed, a hint of excitement in her voice.

As the weight of the situation settled over them, Shelby decided to lighten the mood. "How about we take a break from all this guardian business for a little while? I was thinking of watching a movie. Want to stay and watch with me?"

Travis grinned, happy to see Shelby's relaxed side come out. "I'd love to. What did you have in mind?"

"I was thinking something light and fun, like a romantic comedy," Shelby suggested, heading toward the kitchen. "And what's a movie night without some popcorn?"

Travis followed her, his stomach grumbling at

the mention of the tasty snack. "You read my mind. I'll help you make it."

As they stood side by side in the kitchen, waiting for the popcorn to pop, Shelby felt a strong sense of comfort and belonging. Despite the looming responsibility of being the guardian of the mysterious artifact and the uncertainty of what lay ahead, having Travis by her side made everything feel more manageable.

Harper watched from her perch on the counter, her pretty eyes twinkling with amusement. She knew that Shelby and Travis were meant for each other, and she had a feeling that this adventure would only bring them closer together.

As the popcorn finished popping, Shelby poured it into a large bowl and carried it back to the living room, with Travis following closely behind. They settled on the couch, the light of the television illuminating their faces as they selected a movie.

For a moment, Shelby allowed herself to forget about the mysterious book and the hidden artifact. She focused instead on the comfort of Travis's presence and the simple joy of sharing a movie night with someone she cared about.

Even as they laughed and munched on popcorn, she glanced once at the bookshelf where the book lay hidden, a reminder of the responsibility that had been thrust on her.

As the movie played on, Shelby leaned her head lightly against Travis's shoulder, drawing strength from his warmth and stability. The magic of Hamlet whispered in the air around them, and she knew they would face what lay ahead, one page and one clue at a time.

4

The quaint seaside town of Hamlet was just beginning to stir as the first rays of sunlight crept over the horizon, casting a pretty light over the cobblestone streets. Shelby and her companion, Harper, made their way along Main Street, their footsteps echoing in the early morning stillness.

Their destination was Fiona Medley's shop, a charming little boutique nestled between a cozy café and a vintage clothing store. Known as the "Crow's Crossing," it was a treasure trove of herbs, clothing, jewelry, and spiritual guidance. The shop's large bay windows displayed an array of shimmering crystals, fragrant candles, dresses, and intricately-made bracelets and earrings.

Shelby gently knocked on the door, and a

moment later, Fiona appeared, her warm smile and twinkling eyes radiating a sense of wisdom and kindness. Fiona was a petite woman in her mid-sixties with silvery hair cascading down her shoulders and a face etched with laugh lines that spoke of a life well-lived.

"Shelby, Harper, come in, my dears," Fiona greeted them, ushering them inside the shop. The interior was just as enchanting as the window display, with shelves and racks lined with books, crystals, chic dresses and tops, and unique pieces of jewelry.

Fiona led them to the back room, a cozy space filled with plush armchairs, colorful tapestries, and the soothing aroma of lavender. She motioned for Shelby to take a seat while she prepared a pot of tea, the delicate clinking of China filling the air.

As they settled into their chairs, Harper curled up at Shelby's feet, her ears perked up, ready to listen to the conversation. Shelby took a deep breath, gathering her thoughts before speaking. Fiona set the cups of tea on the table in between them.

"So, tell me your news." The woman took a sip of the fragrant tea.

"Something strange happened at the bookshop yesterday," Shelby began, her voice tinged with apprehension. "A small, mysterious book appeared on one of the display tables, and later in the day, a woman came in looking for a book just like it."

Fiona's eyebrows raised slightly, her interest piqued. "Tell me more about this book. What makes it so special?"

Shelby described the ancient volume, its weathered leather cover, and the peculiar symbols adorning its pages. "At first, the language was completely foreign to me, but when I went back to read the first section, the words somehow translated themselves into English right before my eyes. The first part is the only one that was translated; the other sections are still written in the cryptic language I've never seen."

Fiona leaned forward, her eyes sparkling with intrigue. "And what did section one reveal to you?"

Shelby took a sip of her tea, the warm liquid helping to calm her nerves. "It spoke of a powerful artifact hidden somewhere in Hamlet. The book didn't mention what the artifact was, but it emphasized the importance of keeping it out of the wrong hands. It also referred to a guardian who must protect both the book and the artifact."

She paused, her voice dropping to a near whisper. "The last line of the first section said that the person who possesses the book is its guardian. Fiona, I think that means me."

Harper trilled from her spot on the floor.

Fiona sat back in her chair, a thoughtful expression on her face. She sipped her tea, contemplating Shelby's words. After a moment, with a serious gaze, she looked up at the young woman sitting across from her.

"There have been rumors about this artifact, whispered tales passed down through the decades," Fiona said, her voice low and mysterious. "But it hasn't been seen for almost a century. The rumors say that the book presents itself to a guardian when the artifact is in danger, choosing someone worthy to protect it."

Shelby's heart raced, trepidation coursing through her veins. "So, you don't know what the artifact is either?" she asked, hoping for more information.

Fiona shook her head, a hint of frustration in her eyes. "I'm afraid not. It seems that the knowledge of the artifact's true nature has been lost to time. However..." She paused, a glimmer of an idea forming in her mind.

"Perhaps Magill knows more about it," Fiona suggested, her face brightening with the possibility.

"She's the most powerful psychic in Hamlet, and her knowledge of the town's mystical history is unparalleled. I'll make an appointment for us to meet with her. You, Harper, and I will go together to see what insights she can provide."

Shelby nodded, feeling a sense of relief wash over her. The prospect of having Fiona and Magill's guidance and support in this mysterious adventure brought her a much-needed sense of comfort.

As they continued to sip their tea, Fiona's gaze drifted to the delicate pink quartz pendant resting against Shelby's chest. "Your mother gave you that necklace, didn't she?" she asked, a curious glint in her eyes.

Shelby's fingers instinctively reached for the pendant, a soft smile playing on her lips. "Yes, it's a family heirloom. My mother and grandmother passed it down to me."

Fiona leaned forward, her voice taking on a cryptic tone. "You might want to ask them more about it, Shelby. There might be more to that necklace than meets the eye."

Shelby furrowed her brow, confusion etched on her face. "Why do you say that? What do you mean?"

Fiona took a deep breath, choosing her words carefully. "Your paranormal powers have only revealed themselves in the past six months, and now, just as the artifact is in danger, you have been chosen as its guardian. It's possible that you have a more interesting background than you realize. Talk to your mother and grandmother. They may hold interesting information about your past."

Shelby sat back in her chair, stunned from hearing Fiona's words. She had always known her family had a rich history in Hamlet, but the thought that they might be connected to the mystical world of artifacts and guardians was both thrilling and daunting.

But how could that be true? Her family was a loving, hardworking group of people who supported and cared for each other. There was nothing magical about them.

Harper, sensing Shelby's unease, leapt into her lap, offering a comforting purr, and the young woman stroked the cat's soft fur.

"I'll talk to them," Shelby said. "If there's something they know about our family's history or this necklace, I need to find out. It could be crucial to understanding my skills and my role as a guardian."

Fiona nodded, a proud smile on her face. "You're a brave, smart, and resourceful young woman. I have no doubt you'll unravel the mysteries surrounding the artifact. Remember, Harper and I will be here to help every step of the way."

Shelby smiled at the wise woman sitting before her. Fiona's guidance meant more to her than she could express.

As they finished their tea, Shelby's mind was already racing with a million questions. Fiona walked her and Harper to the front of the shop, the tinkling of wind chimes signaling their departure. As they stepped out onto the sun-dappled street, Shelby felt a sense of purpose. She didn't understand the book, the artifact, or what being a guardian entailed, but she was ready to learn and keep the objects safe from harm.

"I'll let you know as soon as I arrange the meeting with Magill," Fiona said, giving Shelby a warm hug. "In the meantime, trust your instincts. The book chose you for a reason, and I have faith that you'll discover the truth behind the artifact ... and your own legacy."

With a wave goodbye, Shelby and Harper set off down the street, their minds buzzing about the morning conversation. The gentle sea breeze carried the scent of salt and mystery, beckoning them forward on their extraordinary journey.

As they walked, Shelby's hand drifted again to

the pink quartz pendant, feeling its smooth surface beneath her fingertips. She had always cherished it as a symbol of her family's love, but now, she wondered if it held a deeper significance.

The sun climbed a bit higher in the sky as Shelby and Harper walked past the charming storefronts and colorful awnings of Main Street making their way back to the Spellbound Bookshop, eager to unravel the mysteries that lay ahead.

The magic of Hamlet whispered in the air around them, and with a deep breath and a determined smile, Shelby unlocked the door to her beloved bookshop, looking forward to the regular routines and rhythms of the day. When the guardian and her cat stepped inside, Shelby paused for a moment, taking in the familiar sight of the tall shelves and the comforting scent of books.

Harper leapt onto the counter, her tail swishing. "So, what's our next move?" the cat asked, her eyes full of curiosity.

Shelby leaned against the counter, her brow furrowed in thought. "I think we need to start by doing some research. We need to learn more about the history of Hamlet, the rumors surrounding the artifact, and any clues that might help us understand my role as the guardian."

Harper's whiskers twitched with excitement. "And don't forget about your family. If Fiona thinks your mother and grandmother might know something, we should definitely talk to them."

Shelby smiled. "You're right. I'll give them a call later today and see if they can shed some light on this mystery."

As the morning sun streamed through the bookshop's windows, she and Harper exchanged a knowing glance. Together, they would unravel the secrets of the ancient book, discover the truth behind the hidden artifact, and protect the magic that flowed through the heart of Hamlet.

Soon, the bells above the bookshop door jingled, signaling the start of another day.

5

The sun-dappled country road stretched out before Shelby and Harper as they made their way to the Price family's rambling farmhouse on the outskirts of Hamlet. The warm early evening breeze carried the sweet scent of wildflowers and freshly cut grass, a familiar and comforting aroma that reminded Shelby of countless childhood summers spent exploring the fields and orchards surrounding her parents' home.

As the farmhouse came into view, its white clapboard siding and red shutters shining in the afternoon light, Shelby felt a flutter of anticipation in her chest. The conversation with Fiona had left her with a burning desire to uncover her family history and its possible connection to the mysterious book that had fallen into her possession.

Harper, perched comfortably in the passenger seat, looked up at Shelby with knowing eyes. "Are you ready for this?" the cat asked.

Shelby took a deep breath, her fingers tightening on the steering wheel. "As ready as I'll ever be," she replied, a determined smile playing on her lips. "I have a feeling that whatever we learn today could change some things."

As they pulled into the gravel driveway, Shelby's mother, Ginny, and grandmother, Mary, emerged from the farmhouse, their faces lit with warm smiles and open arms. Shelby felt a rush of love wash over her as she stepped out of the car and into their waiting embraces.

"Shelby, it's so nice to see you," Mary exclaimed, her silver hair glinting in the sunlight. "And of course, we can't forget about our favorite feline friend, Harper."

Harper purred contentedly as Mary scratched behind her ears, her eyes shining with affection for the cat.

Ginny, her brown hair streaked with silver, wrapped an arm around Shelby's shoulders and guided her toward the house. "Come on in, sweetheart. I've got a fresh batch of lemonade waiting for us on the porch."

As they settled into the comfortable wicker chairs on the wraparound porch, the gentle hum of bees and the distant lowing of cows creating a peaceful backdrop, Shelby knew it was time to broach the subject that had brought her there.

Reaching up to touch her pink pendant, she turned to her mother and grandmother. "I wanted to talk to you both about my necklace," she began, her voice soft but filled with purpose.

She absent-mindedly rubbed the quartz pendant with her thumb and index finger. "I know my necklace has been passed down through our family for generations, but I recently noticed something unusual about it."

Ginny and Mary exchanged a glance, a flicker of understanding passing between them.

"What did you find?" Mary asked, leaning forward in her chair.

After meeting with Fiona, Shelby had inspected her necklace with a keen eye and spotted something she'd always assumed was a scratch.

She carefully removed the pendant from her

neck and held it out for her mother and grandmother to see. "There's a tiny symbol on the back, one that I always thought was just a scratch, but when I looked closer at it with a magnifying glass, I realized it was written in the same ancient language as a mysterious book that recently came into my possession."

Harper, who had been lounging at Shelby's feet, sat up straight, her ears perked with attention.

Shelby said, "I looked up the symbol. It took me quite a while to find it on the Internet. It means something along the lines of 'To guide and protect the guardian.' I tried to find the meaning of some the other words and symbols, but I couldn't find anything to help me."

Ginny and Mary shared another meaningful look, expressions of surprise and understanding flickering across their faces.

"It seems the time has come," Mary said softly, reaching out to take her daughter's hand in her own. "There's something we need to tell you, Shelby, something about our family history and the role you were born to play. What we have to say might come as quite a shock to you."

As the sun dipped low in the sky, casting long

shadows across the porch, Shelby listened intently as her mother and grandmother wove a tale of magic, secrets, and destiny.

Mary spoke of Susanna, Shelby's great-great-great-grandmother, a woman of extraordinary magical abilities who had been chosen to safeguard a powerful artifact known as the Heart of Hamlet. Susanna had been entrusted with the task of protecting the talisman from those who would seek to use its power for evil.

"The magical ability does not flow from one generation to the next," Mary explained, her voice soft but filled with reverence. "It skips generations until it settles on one young girl in the family tree several generations away from the last magical person. And that girl is you."

Shelby felt a shiver of excitement run down her spine. She had always known that there was something a little different about her, something that set her apart from others, but she had never imagined that it was a destiny written in her family's blood.

"I want to tell you something that happened to me last Christmas," Shelby told them.

Ginny's face took on an expression of concern. "What happened?"

Shelby told them about how she'd fallen from the ladder while decorating the shop, hit her head, fell unconscious for a minute, and then woke up. "I know this might sound strange, but ever since the fall, my intuition has sharpened. I can sometimes also sense things about the future or the past." She looked from her mom to her grandmother who didn't seem alarmed by her revelations.

Grandmother Mary cleared her throat. "We're not surprised to hear this. Some women in our family find their skills when they're children; others find them through an accident or emotional upheaval."

Shelby's eyes were wide. "After what you've told me, it all almost makes sense."

Ginny nodded. "The women of the family wait to see if a daughter develops abilities. If a daughter does develop skills, we explain it as soon as we know. If she doesn't, when she reaches her mid-thirties, we tell her about some of our family members' skills and our history. Your grandmother and I never developed any of the special abilities, but we were taught to look for them in our descendants."

"Do only women in the family develop skills?" Shelby asked.

"Yes," Ginny told her. "In fact, the men don't know anything about it."

Shelby sat quietly for a few moments. "It's a lot to take in, but because I've developed some skills since I fell off the ladder, it feels almost comforting to know some members of our family have experienced the same thing."

Ginny, her eyes shining with love and pride, revealed that the Heart of Hamlet was an ancient talisman imbued with powerful magic, created centuries ago by a coven of witches to protect the town from dark forces and to enhance the skills of town Paranormals. The artifact had been hidden away, its location a closely guarded secret, and the duty of guardianship had been bestowed upon a select few in Shelby's family line.

"Do you know what the artifact is?"

"We don't, but you'll know it when you see it."

Shelby's mind reeled with the weight of the information, her heart pounding hard. She had always felt a deep connection to Hamlet, a sense of belonging that went beyond mere hometown loyalty. Now, she understood why. Her blood was intertwined with the town's mystical history, and she had a sacred duty to uphold it.

"Do you know who's trying to get their hands on the artifact?" Shelby asked.

"We don't know that either," Ginny told her. "I'm sorry we can't be of more help."

Harper, ever the voice of reason, spoke to Shelby's mind, her eyes gleaming with determination. "We'll need all the help we can get," the cat mused, her tail swishing thoughtfully. "Fiona, Magill, and the others ... they'll be invaluable allies in this quest."

Shelby gave a quick nod to the feline. She wasn't ready to reveal to her relatives that she was able to communicate with her cat, but she did tell them all about the appearance of the mysterious book in her shop and that a woman came in asking about a book just like it. She also told her mother and grandmother how she was able to read the first section after it translated itself.

"That's amazing." A second later, Ginny's eyes looked worried. She gave her daughter a weak smile as she wrung her hands in her lap. "Please tell us you'll be careful."

"I will, Mom. I promise."

As the sun began to set, Mary rose from her chair and disappeared into the house, returning moments later with a weathered envelope in her hands.

"A copy of this letter has been passed down from

one magical person to the next in our family," she explained, her voice trembling with emotion. "It contains the information we've just shared with you, Shelby."

Shelby accepted the envelope with reverence, feeling her family's history settling on her shoulders.

As the three generations of women embraced, their hearts full of love and understanding, Shelby felt a surge of gratitude for the extraordinary legacy she had been born into.

Harper rubbed against Shelby's legs, her purr a comforting reminder that she would never be alone on this journey.

As the last rays of the setting sun painted the farmhouse in a warm, golden glow, Shelby and Harper said goodbye to Ginny and Mary. They climbed into the car, the envelope containing the precious letter tucked safely in Shelby's bag, and set off down the country road, back toward the heart of Hamlet and the magical destiny that awaited them.

In the gathering twilight, Shelby felt a sense of calm settle over her. She was the guardian of the Heart of Hamlet, the chosen one tasked with protecting the town and its magical heritage. And with the love of her family, the wisdom of her ancestors, and the support of her friends, both human and feline, she knew that she was ready to face the challenges that lay ahead.

The stars began to wink overhead, their ancient light a reminder of the timeless magic that flowed through Shelby's veins, and as the car wound its way through the countryside, the guardian and her cat set their sights on the future, ready to unravel the mysteries of the past and protect their town.

6

The quiet country road wound through the lush, green landscape of Hamlet, leading Shelby, Harper, and Fiona to the enchanting home of Magill Binney, the most powerful psychic in the area. As they approached the wood-sided house, with its charming thatched roof and glossy, rounded wooden door, Shelby felt a tingle of anticipation run down her spine.

The property was the picture of serenity, with a well-manicured lawn that sparkled in the sunlight, tall trees surrounding the house, and beautiful flower gardens flanking either side of the home. It was as if the very essence of nature's magic had been woven into the fabric of the place.

As they stepped out of the car, the front door of

the cottage opened, and Magill waved to them from the porch. The woman, in her late seventies, had a warm, inviting presence that always put Shelby at ease. Her gray, curly hair fell to her shoulders, framing a face with big, bright eyes that seemed to hold a world of wisdom. Despite her slightly stooped posture, Magill exuded an aura of strength and grace.

"Welcome, my friends," Magill greeted them, her voice soft and melodic. She wore a billowy white blouse and a long blue and white skirt that swayed gently in the breeze. "Please, come in. I've been expecting you."

Shelby, Harper, and Fiona followed Magill through the cozy interior of the house, marveling at the eclectic mix of antiques, crystals, and vases of flowers that adorned the home. The air was thick with the scent of sage and lavender, creating a soothing atmosphere that calmed Shelby's nerves.

Magill led them to a spacious covered porch overlooking the gardens where a table had been set with refreshing juices, a platter of fresh fruits, and a plate of homemade cookies. As they settled into the comfortable wicker chairs, Harper curled up at Shelby's feet, her pretty eyes taking in the tranquil surroundings.

"Now, my dear," Magill began, turning her attention to Shelby, "Fiona tells me that you have come into possession of a most unusual book and that you have been chosen as the guardian of a powerful artifact."

Shelby nodded, her fingers instinctively reaching for her pink quartz pendant. "Yes, somehow the book appeared in my shop, and when I was able to read the first section, it revealed that I'm the guardian of an artifact hidden somewhere in Hamlet. But I don't know what the artifact is, or how to find it. The book is written in a language I don't understand. The day after I found the book, the first section translated itself into English."

Magill listened closely, her face showing understanding. "The artifact has been the subject of much speculation and legend among the magical community," she explained. "What we know about it is a tapestry woven from threads of myth and fact, and discerning one from the other is no easy task."

Fiona, who had been quietly sipping her juice, spoke up. "Magill, have you felt the stirrings of unease among the magical folk? The sense that the artifact may be in danger?"

Magill nodded, her expression growing serious. "Indeed, I have. There has been growing chatter among the Magicals that the artifact is under siege from those who would use its power for their own nefarious purposes. And now, with Shelby revealed as the chosen guardian, it seems the time of reckoning is upon us."

Shelby felt a shiver run over her skin, the weight of responsibility settling heavily on her shoulders. "My mother and grandmother recently told me about our family's connection to paranormal skills and that one of our ancestors, Susanna, was also chosen as a guardian, but they didn't know much about the details."

Magill reached across the table and took Shelby's hand in her own, her touch warm and comforting. "You are part of a long line of Magicals, and you are also descended from several guardians. The magic in your blood has been passed down through generations, waiting for the moment when it would be needed most."

Harper, who had been quietly following the conversation, spoke to Magill's mind, her tail swishing thoughtfully. "But how will Shelby know what to do? The book is still mostly written in a language she can't understand."

Magill smiled, her eyes holding a knowing light. "The translation will come," she told the cat before looking at Shelby. "Trust in the magic that flows through you. The information you seek will be revealed when the time is right."

Shelby sighed, feeling apprehension churning in her gut. "I'm the kind of person who likes to have a plan, to know what steps to take. Not knowing what to do next makes me feel anxious."

Magill nodded, her expression full of empathy. "I understand, but remember, you are not the first guardian to face this challenge, and I suspect you will not be the last. The magic will guide you if you learn to trust in yourself and the power that resides within you."

Fiona reached out and squeezed Shelby's shoulder. "You have already accomplished so much. You have strength and courage that you may not even realize yet. And you have us, your friends and allies, to help you every step of the way."

Shelby was grateful for the women around her and for Harper, her sweet familiar and a source of wisdom and logic. She hoped that with their support, along with the magic that flowed through her veins, she would be ready to face what was to come, but at that moment, she was feeling frightened.

As they continued to talk and share stories, the

afternoon sun began to dip toward the horizon, shining a lovely glow over Magill's enchanting garden. Despite her fears and worries, Shelby felt a sense of peace come over her, a clarity of mind that she hadn't experienced since the mysterious book first appeared in her life.

When it was time to leave, Magill walked them to the door.

"I will confer about the artifact with other Magicals and let you know when I have more information. Remember, Shelby," she said, her voice low, "the artifact will need to be moved to a new hiding place soon. Its current location will be compromised by those who seek to use its power for their own gain. Look to the book for hints and clues, and trust in the magic that guides you. "

Shelby nodded with a determined set to her jaw. "I will. Thank you for everything. I feel like I have a better understanding of what I need to do now, even if I don't have all the answers yet."

As they said their goodbyes and she and Fiona made their way back to the car, Harper looked up at Shelby. "We've got this. Together, we'll find the artifact before it falls into the wrong hands."

Shelby smiled, her heart full of affection for her

feline companion. "You're right. We're a team, and we'll do what needs to be done."

As they drove back toward Hamlet while the sun setting behind them painted the sky in shades of pinks and violets, Shelby knew she would do whatever she could to protect Hamlet's magical legacy.

The road stretched out like a ribbon of possibility, as they drove through the quaint streets of Hamlet. Shelby's mind buzzed with the new information and insights she had gleaned from their meeting with Magill.

Fiona, who had been quietly contemplating the day's events, suddenly spoke up from the passenger seat. "I think it's important that we start researching the history of Hamlet and the legends surrounding the artifact. There may be clues hidden in the town's past that could help us understand its true nature and how to protect it."

Shelby nodded. "You're right. I should start at the library and see what historical records and old newspapers I can find. Maybe there are stories or accounts that mention the artifact or the guardians who came before me."

Harper, who had curled up in the backseat, chimed in, her voice filled with excitement as she spoke to

Shelby's mind. "Don't forget about the ghost in the bookshop. Emily might have some valuable information to share, too. She's been around for a long time and has probably seen and heard things that could help us."

Born in 1890, Emily Harris was the bookstore's resident ghost. When she was twenty-one, the young woman inherited her father's store where the Spellbound Bookshop was now. Rather than sell the small shop her father had built, Emily invested in expanding it into a two-story building and added books and gifts to the shop's inventory. In an age when women rarely participated in business, Emily expanded her father's assets and holdings, and the business thrived.

When she was just twenty-six, a man broke into the shop and attacked her, and Emily died from her injuries. Her spirit never strayed far from the building, wanting to stay close to the place she'd loved in life. The spirit only spoke to Harper, but she'd given the cat messages for Shelby to help her solve a previous cases.

"That's a great idea," Shelby replied to the cat. She needed all the help she could get to navigate this new and mysterious world she found herself in.

She told Fiona, "Thank you for your help. We'll

piece together the puzzle and figure out how to keep the artifact safe."

As they pulled up in front of the Spellbound Bookshop, the streetlights cast a comforting light over the familiar façade. With a deep breath and a smile, Shelby stepped out of the car, ready to begin the next chapter in her adventure as the guardian of the artifact.

7

"I'm not sure about this," Shelby said as she and Lucy walked through town to the community center located on a side lane just off Main Street.

Lucy tried to encourage her friend. "Oh, come on. It'll be fun, and it's something different to do. You might even like it."

"But I don't have any musical experience," Shelby fussed. "I'm going to feel stupid."

"You don't need any experience. The whole thing is casual and relaxed. We're just going to try to create a group rhythm, and it will help us get in tune with ourselves and the other participants. We'll play in a circle to emphasize that we're all equal."

"You said sometimes dancers join in?"

Lucy nodded. "Yeah. Most of the people haven't

had any dance training. They just move to the beat and enjoy the movement and being together."

"I don't know." Shelby was skeptical.

"I've read that drum circles improve memory and attention, and help lessen anxiety and stress," Lucy explained. "Playing with the group promotes relaxation and improves well-being. It even strengthens the immune system, and can heighten creativity."

"It sounds like a wonder drug," Shelby kidded, causing Lucy to laugh.

"When we leave, you'll feel better than when we arrived," Lucy said.

"Yes, I will because it will be over and I can stop worrying about it."

As they approached the community center, Lucy slipped her hand through her friend's arm. "Let's just give it a try. If you don't like it, we won't come back."

"Deal," Shelby agreed.

The community center had a gym, classroom and meeting rooms, a café and lunch room, outdoor walking trails, and a computer room. There were several classes being held that night, and the place was abuzz with people. Lucy and Shelby found their room number on a bulletin board and headed down the hall to the classroom.

Inside, there were different kinds of drums ... djembe, congo, bongo, ashiko, and percussion instruments like shakers and tambourines set out on a long table. Some people had brought their own drums with them. There were about a dozen people who would be taking part.

A woman in her late fifties with chin-length auburn hair welcomed everyone to the class. "Hello, all. I'm Lena Winthrop. I'll be the rhythm facilitator. We're going to play together, connect with each other rhythmically, and take some time for rhythm exploration. I'm so glad you've joined the class. I hope you have fun playing and will make new friends here. Our circle is a worry-free place. Don't be concerned about making a mistake. Just smile and carry on." She gestured to the long table. "Please take a few minutes and try a couple of the drums. Choose the one you'd like to play tonight, then take a seat in the circle."

When everyone was ready, Lena said, "We will start with a warm-up rhythm." She began to play a simple beat, and after repeating it several times, she encouraged the participants to join in. Soon each person was contributing to the sound.

For the next part, Lena suggested they try the call-and-response pattern, where one person plays a rhythm and the others join together to play a complementary rhythm response. Lena started, and though it took several starts and stops accompanied by laughter and encouragement, the others created a response rhythm that was a lot of fun to play.

"Last of all," Lena told them, "we'll end the night with a final rhythm song. We want a lot of enthusiasm and energy to close out our evening." Lena modeled the pattern and they all joined in.

Afterwards, there were refreshments served, and the participants stayed for about twenty minutes to snack and chat with one another.

When Lucy and Shelby left the building and were walking home, Lucy nudged her friend. "So, how did you like it?"

Shelby smiled. "Okay, I admit it was fun. It was energizing and positive. The people were nice. I really enjoyed it."

"That's great. Me, too. You want to continue?"

"I do. Next week, I'm going to choose the bongo drum to play."

∽

After a delightful evening at the drum circle, Shelby bid farewell to Lucy and made her way to the cozy pub where she was meeting Travis. The streetlamps cast a comforting light on the cobblestone streets of Hamlet as she walked, her mind still buzzing with the positive energy and sense of connection she had experienced at the community center.

As she pushed open the wooden door of the pub, Shelby was greeted by the inviting aroma of hearty food and the gentle murmur of conversation. She spotted Travis sitting at a small table in the corner, his handsome features illuminated by the flickering candlelight. He looked up as she approached, a warm smile spreading across his face.

"Hey there, stranger," he said, rising to give her a quick hug. "How was your evening with Lucy?"

Shelby grinned, sliding into the seat opposite him. "It was amazing, actually. Lucy took me to this drum circle at the community center, and I wasn't sure about it at first, but it turned out to be so much fun. The energy, the connection with the other participants ... it was just what I needed."

Travis raised an eyebrow, intrigued. "A drum circle? What is that?"

Shelby explained what went on during the class, and told him about the rhythm sequences they played. "I was really skeptical about going, but it was great. We're going again next week."

"That sounds like quite the experience. I'm glad you enjoyed it. You deserve a break from all the craziness that's been going on lately."

As they settled into easy conversation, ordering drinks and sharing stories, Shelby noticed the way Travis's eyes lingered on her, the chemistry between them crackling like electricity in the air. She felt a flutter of excitement in her chest, a warmth that had nothing to do with the cozy atmosphere of the pub.

But as the evening wore on, Shelby noticed a change in Travis's demeanor. His shoulders seemed to slump, and a frown tugged at the corners of his mouth. She reached across the table, placing her hand gently on his.

"Hey, is everything okay? You seem a little down."

Travis sighed, running a hand through his dark hair. "It's a case I'm working on. I've hit a dead end, and I just can't seem to find the missing piece of the puzzle. It's frustrating, you know? I feel like I'm letting people down, and I'm feeling really tired."

Shelby's heart ached for him, understanding the weight of responsibility he carried as a detective. "Travis, you're an amazing detective. If anyone can solve that case, it's you. Sometimes the answers come when we least expect them. Don't give up."

He gave her a grateful smile, squeezing her hand

in return. "Thanks, Shelby. Your support means a lot to me."

Taking a deep breath, Shelby decided to share the revelation she had recently uncovered about her own family history. "You know, a few days ago, I learned something interesting from my mother and grandmother. Apparently, some of the women in my family have had paranormal abilities, going back generations."

Travis's eyes widened, intrigue flickering across his face. "Really? That's ... wow. I mean, you know I'm from Salem and I have a friend who has some mild paranormal abilities, so the idea isn't a total shock to me. I also know you have incredible intuition and premonitions, but it's still surprising on some level to hear that your ancestors had skills, too." He paused, a soft smile playing on his lips. "I always knew you were special, Shelby Price."

Shelby felt a blush creeping up her cheeks, and a warmth spreading through her chest at his words. "It doesn't bother you, does it? That I have these skills?"

Travis shook his head, his gaze locked with hers. "Not at all. If anything, it makes you even more amazing in my eyes. Your abilities, your compassion, your determination ... they're all part of what makes you who you are. And I happen to think that person is pretty wonderful."

Shelby's heart soared, a rush of emotion washing over her. "Thank you, Travis. That means so much to me."

As they sat there, lost in each other's eyes, the pub seemed to fade away, the world narrowing down to just the two of them. Shelby could feel the magnetic pull between them, the unspoken connection that had been growing stronger with each shared experience and each challenge they faced together.

Travis leaned in closer, his voice low and filled with promise. "Shelby, I..."

Suddenly, the pub door burst open, the sound shattering the intimate moment. A figure stumbled inside, his face obscured by the shadows. Shelby and Travis jumped to their feet, their instincts on high alert.

The man staggered forward, his breath coming in ragged gasps. As he stepped into the light, Shelby's heart nearly stopped. It was Professor Jeffrey Rundle, the expert on medieval texts who taught at the nearby university. She'd wanted to meet with him about the mysterious book to see if he could help decipher the symbols and clues found in its pages.

Something was terribly wrong. Professor Rundle's face was ashen, his eyes wide with terror. He clutched a battered leather backpack to his chest, his knuckles white with the force of his grip.

"Shelby," he rasped when he noticed her, his voice barely above a whisper. "The book ... there is danger. You must..." His words trailed off as he swayed on his feet, his eyes rolling back in his head.

Travis leapt forward, catching the professor before he could collapse to the floor. Shelby rushed to his side, her heart pounding wildly.

"Professor Rundle," she cried, fear and confusion warring within her. "What's happening? What do you mean there's danger?"

But the professor couldn't answer. He had slipped into unconsciousness, his body limp in Travis's arms.

Shelby and Travis exchanged a look of sheer terror, the weight of the professor's words hanging heavy in the air. Somehow, the fate of the mysterious book and the long-lost artifact seemed to hang in the balance, and she feared they were the only ones who could save them.

8

Early in the morning, she met James Peacock at a cozy diner for breakfast. Sitting across from one another sipping coffee, Shelby said, "Please tell me Professor Rundle will be all right."

"Jeffrey will be fine. They'll release him from the hospital in a few days," Mr. Peacock, a friend of the professor, assured her. "He didn't have any injuries. The doctors thought he might have suffered from low blood sugar, low potassium, or perhaps, a mini stroke. They're still doing tests. Jeffrey remembers nothing of the incident. He has no idea how or why he was near the pub that night. I told him he mumbled something about a book and danger, but he has no recollection of saying that and doesn't know what it referred to."

Shelby hung on every word Mr. Peacock said. "An unusual old book showed up in my bookshop on the day of the sale. I called Professor Rundle to set up a meeting with him. I wanted him to take a look at the book and, if he could, tell me something about it."

"You hadn't met with him yet?" Mr. Peacock asked.

"No, we hadn't settled on a convenient time."

"Well, he did speak of a book when he stumbled into the pub. Maybe he meant your book." Mr. Peacock took a bite of his scrambled eggs. "But that might have been on his mind, and in his confusion, random thoughts popped into his head. Anyway, no harm was done, really. He'll be as good as new in a few days."

The topic of conversation shifted to other things, but Shelby still worried that Professor Rundle's episode might somehow be linked to the old, mysterious book in her care.

The workday had been long and peculiar for Shelby with an unshakable feeling of unease clinging to her like a second skin. As she went about her tasks in the bookshop, her mind kept drifting to the mysterious old book hidden away in her apartment. When lunchtime finally arrived, she and Harper eagerly climbed the stairs, hoping to find that the next section had miraculously translated itself, just like the first. But, as they carefully opened the ancient tome, their hearts sank as the pages remained covered in the indecipherable, ancient script.

"I don't understand," Shelby murmured, her fingers gently tracing the strange words. "Why isn't it translating like it did before? Do you think we did something wrong?" she asked Harper.

The cat tilted her head as her gaze fixed on the book. "I don't think so. Maybe the book has its own timeline, revealing its secrets when it deems fit. We have to trust the process, as Magill said."

Disappointed but not deterred, Shelby returned to the bookshop, the weight of the artifact's secrets pressing heavily on her shoulders. As the day wore on and the sun began to set, sending long shadows across the quaint streets of Hamlet, Shelby finally closed up the shop and made her way back to her cozy apartment.

Determined to unlock the mysteries hidden

within the book, she called on her trusted friends Lucy and Travis to join her and Harper in her kitchen. When the three people settled around the table, the air felt thick with anticipation as Shelby told them how frustrated she'd been feeling.

"I've felt antsy and uneasy all day. I keep thinking about this book. I have to figure out where the artifact is so I can move it to a safe place. If I don't get clues from the book, I won't be able to find it."

"I think the book will give you a clue tonight," Lucy told her friend. "I bet that's why you've been on edge all day."

Shelby looked downtrodden.

"Why does the artifact have to be moved?" Lucy asked.

With a shrug, Shelby replied, "I don't know exactly. Magill told me that over time, the artifact starts to lose its power and has to be moved to a new hiding place to regain its strength. I don't have many details."

"Bring the book out," Travis suggested. "Let's see if the words and symbols have been translated yet."

With a sigh, Shelby stood and left the room. When she returned, she was carrying the mysterious old book. She set it on the table and stared at it.

Then with a deep breath, she carefully opened the cover and turned to the next section. "Oh, my gosh!"

To their amazement and delight, the pages of the next section began to shimmer and shift, the ancient words morphing and rearranging themselves until they formed words and sentences in English. The small group leaned in closer, their eyes widening as they began to read the cryptic clues and riddles that promised to lead them on a treasure hunt across the picturesque town of Hamlet.

"It seems there's a series of clues we need to follow," Shelby said.

The first clue spoke of "a place where knowledge is kept, and the past is preserved," and a flicker of recognition danced in Travis's eyes. "Of course, the library," he said, his voice full of excitement. "That's got to be the first stop on our hunt."

Lucy nodded, her blonde hair bouncing from her enthusiasm. "It makes sense. The library is the heart of Hamlet's history and knowledge. If there are secrets to be found, that's where we'll find them."

The group set off into the night, their footsteps echoing against the cobblestone streets as they made their way toward the Hamlet Public Library. The building loomed before them, its stately façade bathed in the gentle glow of the streetlamps, and Shelby felt a thrill of anticipation as they climbed the steps and pushed open the heavy wooden doors.

Inside, the library was a labyrinth of tall shelves and hushed whispers, the scent of books hanging heavy in the air. The group split up, each taking a different section of the library to search for anything that might relate to the clue.

As Shelby wandered through the stacks carrying Harper under her jacket, she had the eerie feeling that they were being watched. She glanced over her shoulder, half-expecting to see a shadowy figure lurking among the shelves, but there was no one there. Shaking off the odd sensation, she continued her search, her eyes scanning the titles and covers for any hint of the puzzle piece they were looking for.

"Find anything yet?" Lucy whispered, appearing suddenly at Shelby's side, her blue eyes wide with curiosity.

Shelby shook her head, a frown tugging at her lips. "Not yet. It's like looking for a needle in a haystack. This library is huge, and we don't even know what we're searching for."

Lucy gave her friend a reassuring smile,

squeezing her arm gently. "We'll find it. We have to. The artifact depends on us."

Meanwhile, Travis found himself drawn to the local history section, his keen detective skills guiding him toward a large, old painting that hung on the wall. The canvas depicted a scene from Hamlet's early days with horse-drawn carriages and women in elegant gowns strolling along the main street. As Travis examined the painting more closely, his heart skipped a beat as he noticed a small symbol hidden within the brushstrokes, almost invisible to the eye. He studied the symbol, recognizing it as one of the same ones found in the mysterious book.

Excitement bubbled up in his chest as he hurried to find the others. His overly loud voice echoed through the library's hushed halls when he spotted the two young women. "I found something. Come see it."

Shelby and Lucy gathered around the painting, their faces full of curiosity as Travis pointed out the hidden symbol. Lucy, her eyes narrowed in concentration, pulled out a small notebook and carefully copied the symbol, her pencil scratching against the paper in the silence of the library.

Encouraged by their discovery, they turned their attention to the next clue, which had been cleverly woven into the painting itself. As they worked together to decipher the cryptic message, Harper's tail twitched with anticipation, her feline senses heightened by the thrill of the hunt.

"I think I've got it," Travis said, his voice low and urgent. "Look at the books in the painting. See what's written on the covers. The words: 'eternal rest' and 'forgotten names.' I bet it's leading us to the old cemetery on the outskirts of town."

With a wide smile, Shelby nodded, excitement running down her back. "The cemetery ... where the town's history is quite literally buried. It makes sense that the next piece of the puzzle would be hidden among the gravestones." She squeezed Travis's hand. "Well done. No wonder you're such a great detective."

The clue did indeed lead them to the old cemetery on the outskirts of Hamlet, where weathered gravestones stood sentinel beneath the inky black sky. The group split up once again, their flashlights cutting through the darkness as they searched for the next clue.

Harper moved quickly under the moonlight, and suddenly, she let out a soft meow, drawing the others to a particular gravestone. As they huddled around the marker, their breath clouding in the cool night air, Shelby's heart raced as she spotted another hidden symbol etched into the stone, almost invisible to the naked eye.

With trembling fingers, she reached out and traced the symbol, a sense of foreboding washing over her. The clues were leading them deeper into the heart of Hamlet's mysteries, but to what end?

"I don't like this," Lucy whispered, her voice trembling slightly as she huddled closer to Shelby. "This place gives me the creeps, especially at night. It's like we're disturbing something that's meant to stay buried."

Travis placed a comforting hand on Lucy's shoulder, his eyes scanning the shadowy cemetery for any signs of danger. "I don't see anything that will put us in danger. We're getting closer. We can't stop now. Whatever secrets this town holds, we have to uncover them if we want to protect the artifact and keep Hamlet safe."

As the night wore on and the clues grew more complex, the group found themselves at a loss, unable to decipher the meaning behind the symbol and the gravestone. Exhausted and frustrated, they decided to call it a night, vowing to regroup the next day with fresh eyes and renewed determination.

As they made their way back through the streets

of Hamlet, each lost in their own thoughts, Shelby again had the feeling that they were being watched. She glanced all around, but the streets were nearly empty, showing only the occasional flicker of a streetlamp.

When they finally reached Shelby's apartment, the three of them collapsed onto the couches and chairs, their minds pondering the events of the night. Harper curled up in Shelby's lap, her purrs a soothing balm to the young woman's frayed nerves.

"We're getting closer," Travis said, his voice low and determined. "I know it. We just need to keep pushing forward."

Lucy and Shelby nodded in agreement.

"We should get some rest," Shelby said, stifling a yawn as she glanced at the clock on the wall. "Tomorrow's a new day, and we'll need all our energy and wits about us if we're going to solve this mystery and find the artifact before it's too late."

With hugs and goodbyes, Lucy and Travis headed out to their own homes.

With the moon's light shining through her bedroom window, Shelby drifted off to sleep, her dreams haunted by the mysteries of Hamlet and the secrets hidden within the pages of the ancient book. The treasure hunt was far from over, and the next clue might lead them deeper into the darkness, where ancient magic and modern evil collided in a battle.

But for now, she slept, her heart full of hope. She and her companions had taken the first steps on a journey to protect their town, and they would continue to their goal, one hidden clue at a time.

9

The Hamlet Historical Society's library could be a treasure trove of information, its shelves lined with old books, yellowed newspapers, and delicate manuscripts that whispered of the town's rich and mysterious past. Shelby and Lucy stepped through the heavy doors, the scent of old paper enveloping them like a warm embrace.

The librarian, a petite woman with silver hair and bright, inquisitive eyes, greeted them with a warm smile. "Welcome. How may I assist you today?"

Shelby took a deep breath, her heart fluttering with anticipation. "We're looking for information about my family's history in Hamlet. I recently discovered that some of my ancestors may have been involved in the town's supposed mystical past, and I'm hoping to learn more."

The librarian's eyes sparkled with intrigue. "Ah, a family mystery. That can be a thrilling road to discovery. Let's see what we can uncover together. Follow me."

She led them through the labyrinth of shelves, the antique lamps casting a warm light on the faded spines of some of the books. Shelby and Lucy exchanged a glance, their footsteps echoing softly on the polished wooden floor.

As they walked, Shelby marveled at the sheer volume of information contained within the walls. Each book, each document, and each photograph held a piece of Hamlet's history, a fragment of the stories that had shaped the town and its people over the centuries. She felt a sense of awe, a deep connection to the past that she'd rarely experienced before.

"Here we are," the librarian announced, gesturing to a section marked *Hamlet's Arcane History*. "If your ancestors were indeed involved in the town's 'magical' heritage..." She used her fingers to mimic quotation marks around the word *magical* before finishing her sentence. "This is where you'll find what you're looking for."

Shelby and Lucy set to work, carefully leafing

through the delicate pages of old diaries, council records, and secret society manifestos. The hours ticked by, the world outside the library fading away as they lost themselves in the fascinating tales of Hamlet's past.

As they read, Shelby felt a sense of kinship with the men and women who had walked these streets before her, the brave souls who had dedicated their lives to protecting the magic that flowed through Hamlet's veins. Their stories, their sacrifices, resonated deep within her, a testament to the unbreakable bonds of family, friends, and community.

As Shelby read over a particularly old and fragile document, her breath caught in her throat.

"Lucy, look at this," she whispered, her voice trembling with excitement. "It's a record of a secret society called the Guardians of Hamlet. And look here ... some of the names listed are my ancestors."

Lucy leaned in, her eyes widening as she scanned the faded ink. "The Guardians were dedicated to preserving Hamlet's magical heritage and protecting a certain item from falling into the wrong hands. Shelby, this is incredible. Your family has been watching over the town's secrets for generations."

Shelby felt a surge of pride and responsibility wash over her, a sense of connection to her ancestors that she had never experienced before, but as she continued to read, her heart started to sink, a chill creeping up her spine.

"Wait ... there's more," she said, her voice barely above a whisper. "One of my ancestors, a woman named Esmeralda, turned to dark magic. She tried to harness the magical power for herself, betraying the Guardians and nearly destroying Hamlet in the process."

Lucy gasped. "Wow. This is a lot to take in, but every family has a black sheep or two."

Shelby nodded. "I need to know more. I have to understand what happened; why Esmeralda turned her back on her own people."

The librarian, who had just come back into the room spoke up, her voice soft and filled with understanding. "The path to the truth is rarely an easy one, but I have a feeling that the answers you seek may lie within the pages of Esmeralda's personal diary. It's a fragile text, but I believe it could be helpful in understanding your family's past. There's an epilogue at the end of the diary written by someone other than Esmeralda."

With trembling hands, Shelby put on soft gloves

as the librarian placed the weathered leather-bound book on the table in front of her. She and Lucy exchanged a determined glance.

As they settled into their seats with the soft golden light of the lamps illuminating the pages before them, Shelby began to read, her heart pounding with excitement.

Esmeralda's words, penned in an elegant, flowing script, painted a vivid picture of a woman torn between her duty to the Guardians and her own insatiable hunger for power. She wrote of the seductive whispers of dark magic, the temptation to wield the artifact's energy for her own gain, and the bitter price she paid for her betrayal.

As Shelby delved deeper into Esmeralda's story, she felt a sense of empathy for her ancestor despite the darkness of her actions. Esmeralda's words spoke of a woman who had once been filled with hope and light, a woman who had dreamed of using her powers to make the world a better place. But somewhere along the way, she had lost sight of what really mattered, allowing her ambition and her ego to consume her.

Reaching the epilogue written by someone other than Esmeralda, Shelby felt tears prickling at the corners of her eyes, a heavy sadness washing over her as she read of the betrayal that had nearly torn Hamlet apart, with the Guardians fighting desperately to protect the town and keep the artifact from Esmeralda's dark intentions.

"She was stopped," Shelby whispered, her voice thick with emotion. "Two Guardians ... they managed to defeat her and banish the dark magic from Hamlet, but the cost... the cost was high. Esmeralda was killed."

Lucy placed a comforting hand on Shelby's shoulder. "They sacrificed so much to keep the town safe, to protect the magic that flows through it. And now... now it's up to you to carry on their legacy, to ensure that their efforts weren't in vain."

Shelby nodded, a fierce determination burning in her chest. "I won't let them down. I won't let Esmeralda's mistakes define my family's legacy. We'll find the artifact, and we'll protect it, no matter what it takes."

As they sat there, surrounded by the whispers of the past, Shelby and Lucy realized they were part of something bigger than themselves. They had to protect the magic that had endured for generations.

The librarian came back into the room and walked over to the young women's table. "These archives hold a great deal of information about the town's supposed magical community. It's up to the reader to decide what's true and what isn't. Some people believe in such things, and some don't. You have to decide for yourselves," she said, her voice soft. She gave them a knowing look. "I have no doubt that you'll meet the future with courage and grace."

Shelby felt a surge of affection for the kind-hearted librarian. "Thank you," she whispered, her voice trembling with emotion. "Thank you for helping us with all of this."

The librarian smiled. "I'm happy to do it. The Hamlet Historical Society has always been a haven for people seeking knowledge and understanding. I see in you a strong spirit with a fierce determination to protect and preserve our little town, where all people are welcome."

As Shelby and Lucy gathered their notes and prepared to leave the library, they paused to look at the rows of books that stretched out before them, some of which were a testament to the power of story and the bonds of community.

"You know," Lucy said softly, "I've always felt there was something special about Hamlet, something that set it apart from other places, but I never imagined its magical history was real, that there was a whole hidden world of mystery and power lurking just beneath the surface."

Shelby nodded, a smile tugging at the corners of her lips. "I know what you mean. It's like we've been given a glimpse behind the curtain, a chance to be part of something important."

With a final nod of thanks to the librarian, they stepped out into the sunlit streets of Hamlet. The legacy of the Guardians, of the brave men and women who had sacrificed to protect the magic of Hamlet, lived on, and they would do all they could to keep the artifact safe and the town secure.

"Too bad there were no clues about what and where the artifact is hidden," Lucy said to her friend.

"I guess that's because it would make it too easy for people with ill intentions to find."

"That makes sense," Lucy agreed.

"We'll have to figure it out on our own." Shelby paused for several moments before adding, "I'm unclear what will happen if the artifact falls into the wrong hands. I know it would be bad, but what would the outcome be? We don't even know who we're fighting. How can we hide it from unknown enemies?"

"Magill didn't tell you anything about who wants

the artifact? She didn't mention what will happen if it falls into the wrong hands?"

"She didn't. She's trying to figure it out."

Lucy kidded, "Maybe she's afraid you'll run for the hills if you find out how bad it could get. Maybe she doesn't want to scare you."

Shelby looked at Lucy with wide eyes. "Thanks a lot for planting that idea in my head." She bopped her friend on the arm.

The two continued down Main Street, preparing to unravel the mysteries of the past and protect the magic of their sweet little town.

10

The sun had just begun to set over the quaint town, casting an eerie glow across the rooftops and trees. Shelby, Travis, and Lucy sat around the small dining table in Shelby's cozy apartment, the remnants of their dinner scattered before them. Harper, ever-present and watchful, perched on the windowsill, scanning the darkening streets below.

"So, what do we know so far?" Travis asked, his forehead lined in concentration. "We've got a mysterious book, a hidden artifact, and a bunch of cryptic clues that seem to be leading us on a wild goose chase across town."

Shelby nodded, her fingers absently tracing the edges of the old book that lay on the table before her. "And don't forget there's someone, or multiple someones, who are trying to beat us to the prize."

Lucy shuddered, her eyes wide with worry. "I don't like the thought of going up against them. They must be really dangerous."

"We don't have a choice," Shelby said, her voice low and determined. "If we don't find the artifact first, who knows what they'll do with it? We have to protect Hamlet, no matter what."

Harper leapt down from the windowsill, her tail swishing as she spoke to Shelby's mind. "I think our next step should be to go back to the cemetery. There was something about that gravestone that felt important, like it was trying to tell us something."

Because Travis didn't know that the cat could communicate with Shelby, she pretended the idea was her own. "I think we need to go back to the old cemetery."

Travis and Lucy exchanged a glance, their faces etched with uncertainty.

"The cemetery? At night, again? Are you sure that's a good idea?" Lucy asked, her voice trembling slightly.

Shelby reached across the table, giving her friend's hand a quick, reassuring squeeze. "I know it's scary, but I think we have to do it. We're the only ones who can solve this mystery and keep the artifact safe. We'll be watchful and careful. It will be harder for anyone to track us in the dark."

Travis nodded, his jaw set with determination. "Shelby's right. We can't back down now. Let's head to the cemetery and see if we can decipher that clue."

As the three friends and the cat made their way through the darkened streets of Hamlet, the shadows seemed to lengthen and twist, as if reaching out to grab them. The moon hung low in the sky, casting a cold silver light across the cobblestones and the trees.

Suddenly, Harper stopped short, her fur standing on end. "Wait," she hissed to Shelby, her eyes darting back and forth. "I heard something."

"Stop," Shelby told the others. "Did you hear that?"

The group froze, their hearts pounding. The sound of footsteps echoed in the distance, growing closer with each passing second.

"It might be them," Shelby whispered, her voice tight with fear. "The dark magic practitioners. They must have followed us here."

Travis grabbed Shelby's hand, his eyes blazing with intensity. "We have to move. We can't let them catch us, but let's not be obvious that we're on to them. Walk fast, but don't run."

The four took off through the dark, their feet moving fast against the pavement as they hurried through the twisting streets and alleys of Hamlet. The footsteps behind them seemed to grow louder, but they couldn't be sure if it was someone following them or just people innocently walking around the town.

At last, they reached the gates of the old cemetery, the wrought-iron bars looming before them like the jaws of some great beast.

"The gate is latched tonight." Shelby's hands shook as she fumbled with it, the metal cold and unyielding beneath her fingers.

"Hurry," Lucy whispered, her eyes wide with terror. "I hear footsteps again."

With a few desperate tugs, the gate swung open, and they stumbled inside, their chests heaving with exertion. The ancient cemetery stretched out before them, a sea of crumbling gravestones and gnarled trees. The shadows seemed to dance and writhe in the moonlight.

"Maybe we should hide, just in case," Shelby told them, her eyes searching around for somewhere to take refuge.

Travis grabbed the young women's arms and tugged them. "There's an old mausoleum down this lane. I noticed the door was partially open the last time we were here."

Hurrying down the lane, they reached the mausoleum and stepped into its cold dark interior. When they hunched down in the corner, Travis placed his hand on the revolver he'd hidden under his pant leg. "Quiet now," he told the women.

They heard footsteps coming toward them and held their breath. Whoever it was stopped walking and stood unmoving for several seconds just outside the mausoleum.

Lucy reached for Shelby's hand. The friends waited, daring not to make a sound.

After what seemed like an hour but was really only minutes, the footsteps moved away until they couldn't hear them anymore. Shelby, Travis, Lucy, and Harper stayed still and quiet for another fifteen minutes, afraid their pursuers might come back. The hoot of an owl made Shelby jump.

"Where's the grave we found last time?" Travis finally asked. "We need to find that clue and get out of here before they come back to find us."

Shelby closed her eyes, trying to remember the location of the mysterious gravestone. "I think I remember where it is," she said at last, her voice trembling slightly. "Let's go."

As they picked their way through the overgrown grass, Shelby recalled the sound of their pursuers' footsteps, the thud of their shoes against the earth that had sent shivers down her spine.

Harper darted ahead, her feline senses guiding them toward the grave they were trying to find.

"Here," Shelby said, her voice soft in the dark and eerie stillness of the cemetery. "Harper found it."

Shelby, Travis, and Lucy huddled around the weathered stone, their eyes straining to make out the faded inscription in the dim light of their flashlight. The symbol they had discovered earlier was etched into the rough surface like a silent guardian.

"What does it mean?" Lucy whispered, her voice trembling with fear. "How is this supposed to help us find the artifact?"

Shelby traced the lines of the symbol with her finger, her mind racing. "It's definitely a clue," she said at last. "It's just a puzzle we need to solve."

Travis leaned in closer, his brow lined in concentration. "Look," he said, pointing to a series of small, almost invisible markings around the edges of the symbol. "Those look like numbers. Could they be coordinates, maybe?"

Shelby's eyes widened, a flicker of hope igniting in her chest. "You're right," she breathed, her voice filled with excitement. "If we can figure out those coordinates, they might lead us to the artifact's hiding place."

But before they could begin to unravel the clue, the sound of voices pierced the night air, sending a jolt of fear through their veins. Were the dark magic practitioners coming back?

Shelby noticed two shadowy figures, a man and a woman, moving through the darkness like wraiths. For a second, peering through the trees, she thought the woman seemed familiar.

"Hurry," Travis shouted, grabbing Shelby's hand and pulling her away from the grave. "We have to get out of here, now."

They took off running, weaving through the maze of gravestones and monuments as the sound of their pursuers' footsteps seemed to grow closer. Shelby's heart pounded, the blood rushing in her ears as she gasped for breath.

Suddenly, Harper let out a sharp hiss, her fur bristling with fear. "Are they cutting us off?" she cried, her voice filled with panic.

Shelby looked around wildly, her eyes searching for some means of escape. Were the evil-doers closing in on them?

Travis's eyes fell on a small, half-hidden path that wound its way through the perimeter of the cemetery, disappearing into the shadows of the trees beyond.

"This way," he told them with urgency. "Follow me."

Plunging into the darkness, the branches of the trees tore at their clothing and skin as they ran.

Minutes later, Shelby, Travis, Lucy, and Harper collapsed against the trunk of a large oak tree, their chests heaving with exertion and relief.

"That was way too close," Lucy whispered, the sound of her voice revealing how close she was to crying. "We can't keep doing this. It's too dangerous."

Shelby nodded, her heart still racing. "I know," she said softly, "but I can't give up. I have to find the artifact before they do."

"You know I won't abandon you," Lucy told her with a shake of her head, "even though I'd like to. Did either of you see their faces?"

"I thought I recognized the woman," Shelby admitted, "but I was too focused on getting away from them."

"I didn't see them either." Travis pulled out his phone, his fingers flying across the screen as he entered the coordinates they had deciphered from the gravestone. "I think I know where we need to go next," he told them. "We need to be very careful. They'll be watching for us now."

Harper rubbed against Shelby's leg, her purr a comforting presence in the darkness.

"The whole thing scares me to death, but we can do this," Shelby said. The sound of her voice was filled with quiet confidence. "We're the only ones who can. Magill taught me a protection spell, but I'm not good at it yet. I'll keep trying to improve so I can help us stay safe."

"Good. That will be a big help." Travis stood and helped the two young women to their feet. "Come on. Let's get out of here."

With a final, determined nod, they set off into the night, ready to follow the trail of clues that would lead them to the artifact. The dark magic practitioners might be hot on their heels, but despite their fear and worry, Shelby and her friends would not be stopped.

11

The morning sun shined through the windows of the Spellbound Bookshop, illuminating the cozy interior with its soft light. Shelby moved about the shop, her mind still focused on the events of the previous night. What felt like a narrow escape from the dark magic practitioners in the cemetery had left her shaken but more determined than ever to unravel the mysteries surrounding the ancient book and the hidden artifact.

As she busied herself with the usual morning tasks, straightening displays and greeting early customers, the door opened, signaling a new arrival. Shelby looked up, a welcoming smile on her face, but the sight of the woman standing in the doorway made her blood run cold.

Evelyn Blackwell, the historian who had shown such a keen interest in finding an old, mysterious book stood before her, her dark eyes glinting with an expression Shelby couldn't quite figure out.

"Good morning, Ms. Price," Evelyn said, her voice smooth and cultured, with just a hint of an accent. "I hope I'm not interrupting anything."

Shelby swallowed hard, trying to calm the sudden racing of her heart. "Not at all, Ms. Blackwell."

Evelyn stepped further into the shop, her gaze sweeping over the shelves and displays with a calculating air. "I was just wondering if you'd had a chance to check your offsite storage area for that old book I inquired about. You remember, the one with the unusual symbol on the cover?"

Shelby felt a bead of sweat trickle down the back of her neck, her mind spinning as she tried to come up with a plausible explanation. "I apologize, Ms. Blackwell. I've been meaning to get in touch with you about that. I'm afraid the book is no longer in our inventory. It seems to have been misplaced or perhaps sold without being properly logged."

Evelyn's eyes narrowed, a flicker of suspicion passing over her face. "Is that so? How unfortunate. I don't suppose any of your employees might recall seeing it or making an entry about it?"

Shelby shook her head, hoping her expression appeared suitably apologetic. "I'm sorry, but no one seems to remember anything about it. We've searched high and low, but it's simply not here anymore. Maybe there was some sort of glitch in the inventory software."

Evelyn studied Shelby for a long moment, her gaze intense and probing. "Very well. I suppose these things do happen from time to time."

As Shelby tried to think of a response, a sudden flicker of recognition passed through her mind. The way Evelyn held herself ... it reminded her of the shadowy figure she had seen in the cemetery the night before. Could Evelyn have been one of the dark magic practitioners pursuing them?

As if reading her thoughts, Evelyn tilted her head, a small, knowing smile playing at the corners of her mouth. "Tell me, were you out walking last evening? I thought I caught a glimpse of you near the old cemetery at the edge of town."

Shelby's heart skipped a beat, her palms growing clammy with fear. She forced herself to meet Evelyn's gaze and keep her voice steady and calm. "I'm afraid you must be mistaken. I was here at the shop late into the evening, taking care of some paperwork. Maybe it was someone who looked like me."

Evelyn's smile widened, but there was no warmth in her eyes. "Perhaps," she murmured, her tone laced with a hint of skepticism.

Shelby straightened and took in a long breath. "Why were you out near the old cemetery?"

Evelyn stared at the young woman for a few moments. "I like to take long walks when I need to clear my head." She squared her shoulders. "Well, should the book happen to make an appearance, please do give me a call. I would be most grateful."

With that, Evelyn turned and strode out of the shop, the bell above the door jingling in her wake. Shelby let out a shaky breath, her knees suddenly weak with relief.

Harper, who had been watching the exchange from her perch atop a nearby bookshelf, leapt down and hurried over to Shelby.

"That was close," Harper murmured. "Do you think she knows something? Could she be involved with the dark magic practitioners?"

Shelby ran a hand through her long brown hair, her brain buzzing. "I don't know. There's something about her that doesn't sit right with me, but I can't quite put my finger on it."

She began to pace the length of the shop, her eyes narrowed. "On the one hand, she seems genuinely interested in the book, like maybe she's trying to help protect it. But on the other hand, the way she looked at me just now... it was like she could see right through me, like she knew I was lying."

Harper nodded, her tail swishing back and forth with agitation. "We need to be careful. If Evelyn is involved with the dark forces seeking the artifact, she could be a dangerous enemy, but if she's an ally, someone who wants to keep the book and the artifact safe, we could use her help."

Shelby sighed, the weight of the mystery pressing down on her like a physical burden. "I wish I knew what to do. I feel like we're stumbling around in the dark, trying to put together a puzzle with half the pieces missing."

The cat leapt up onto the counter, her eyes shining with encouragement. "Don't despair. We'll figure it out. We're making progress."

Shelby managed a small smile, drawing strength from her sweet cat friend. "You're right, Harper. We're getting closer."

She glanced toward the window, watching as the

tourists walked by and the people of Hamlet went about their daily lives, unaware of the ancient magic and dark forces swirling just beneath the surface of their quaint little town.

"We'll meet with Travis later this evening. He thinks he knows what those coordinates we found on the gravestone lead to." Her voice sounded low and determined.

Harper nodded, her whiskers twitching. "And we should keep an eye on Evelyn, too. See if we can figure out what her true intentions are."

Shelby felt a flicker of unease at the thought of the mysterious historian, but she pushed it aside, focusing instead on the task at hand. "Agreed. We'll need to be careful. If she is working with the dark practitioners, we can't let her know what we're up to."

As the two friends planned their next move, Shelby thought about how the ancient book sometimes seemed to hum with a strange energy, as if sensing the growing urgency of their quest.

With a nod, Shelby said, "Maybe tonight when we meet Travis, we'll find the next clue, but first, there's something we have to do."

Myths and Magic

As the sun began to dip toward the horizon, Shelby and Harper made their way to Magill's enchanting cottage on the outskirts of Hamlet. The revelations about her family's legacy and the impending threat of the dark magic practitioners weighed heavily on her mind.

Fiona greeted her at the door, her warm smile and twinkling eyes a welcome sight after the tensions of the day. "Come in," she said, ushering Shelby and Harper into the cozy living room where Magill waited, seated in a plush armchair by the fireplace.

The older psychic looked up as Shelby entered, her gaze sharp and penetrating. "I sensed your arrival," she said, with a melodic tone. "The spirits whisper of great challenges ahead, but also of the strength and courage that lies within you."

Shelby felt a shiver run down her spine at Magill's words, but she stood straight and tall. "I'm ready to learn," she said, her voice steady and strong. "I know I have to be prepared to defend against the dark forces that seek to control the artifact."

Magill nodded, a small smile playing at the corners of her mouth. "Your ancestors would be proud of you. You carry their strength and wisdom within you, even if you don't yet fully realize it."

Fiona placed a gentle hand on Shelby's shoulder, her touch warm and friendly in the dimly lit room. "Magill and I will teach you the techniques and spells that have been passed down through generations."

As the flames flickered in the hearth and the scent of sage and lavender filled the air, Shelby worked on her training, her mind and body focused on the tasks at hand.

Magill and Fiona were patient and wise teachers, guiding Shelby through the intricacies of magical defense and the channeling of her own innate powers. They'd taught her how to create protective wards and shields, how to deflect dark spells and curses, and how to tap into the energy of the earth itself to bolster her own strength.

At first, Shelby struggled with the unfamiliar techniques, her movements clumsy and uncertain, but as time passed and the lessons continued, she began to feel a change within herself, a growing sense of confidence and power that seemed to flow from the core of her being.

Fiona watched with pride as Shelby mastered a particularly difficult shielding spell, her eyes shining with admiration. "You're a natural," she said, her voice filled with warmth. "The magic is strong within you, just as it was with your ancestors."

Shelby felt a flush of pride at Fiona's words, but she knew she still had much to learn. "I just hope it will be enough," she said, her brow furrowed with concern. "I have a lot to learn in a short time. I know the dark magic practitioners are powerful, and they'll stop at nothing to get their hands on the artifact."

Magill rose from her chair, her movements slow but graceful. With her voice filled with quiet conviction, she said, "You have the strength of your friends and family behind you, and the wisdom of the ages to guide you."

She placed a gnarled hand on Shelby's forehead, her touch cool and soothing. "Close your eyes, child," she murmured, her voice barely above a whisper. "Let the magic flow through you. Let it become part of you."

Shelby did as she was told, her eyes fluttering closed as she felt a strange, tingling sensation begin to spread through her body. It was as if a warm, golden light was filling her from within, chasing away the shadows of doubt and fear that had been clinging to her.

As she stood there, lost in the embrace of the

ancient magic, Shelby saw visions flash before her mind's eye, glimpses of the past and the future intertwined. She saw her ancestors, brave and strong, standing against the forces of darkness with the power of the artifact at their command. She saw herself, older and wiser, leading a new generation of Magicals in the fight against evil.

And she saw the town of Hamlet, its streets filled with light and laughter, and the magic that flowed through it protected and cherished by those who called it home.

When at last the visions faded and Shelby opened her eyes, she found herself surrounded by a soft, shimmering aura, the air around her crackling with energy.

Magill and Fiona stood before her, their faces filled with hope.

"The magic has chosen you," Magill said, her voice full of emotion. "You are the guardian, the one who will protect the artifact."

As the three women embraced and Harper rubbed her head against their legs, their hearts filled with hope and unity, and Shelby knew she was exactly where she was meant to be.

The training would continue on another day with Magill and Fiona imparting their wisdom and knowledge. She knew the true test of her abilities was still to come, that the dark magic practitioners planned to claim the artifact for their own.

As she stepped out into the night, Shelby felt a sense of calm wash over her, and with a grateful glance back at the cottage and the two extraordinary women who had become her mentors and her friends, she set off toward town with Harper, the magic of Hamlet humming in the air around her.

12

As the sun began to set over the town, Shelby sat on the sofa in her cozy apartment, her mind still unsettled from the revelations of the past few days. The ancient book, the hidden artifact, and the dark magic practitioners who sought to claim it for their own—it was all so much to take in, but she knew she couldn't afford to let her guard down, not even for a moment.

A knock at the door startled her from her thoughts, and she felt a flutter of excitement in her chest as she realized who it must be. She opened the door to find Travis standing there, a warm smile on his face and a bag of groceries in his hand.

"I thought you could use a home-cooked meal,"

he said, his eyes twinkling with affection. "I bet you haven't eaten. How about we cook together?"

Shelby felt a rush of warmth wash over her as she stepped aside to let him in. "You have no idea how much I needed this," she said, her voice soft.

As Travis set about unpacking the groceries and preparing their meal, Shelby watched him, admiring the ease with which he moved about her small kitchen. There was something about his presence that made her feel safe and grounded, even in the midst of all the chaos and uncertainty that swirled around them.

Harper, who had been dozing on the windowsill, perked up at the sound of Travis's voice, her face shining with curiosity. She jumped down and wound herself around his legs, purring contentedly as he reached down to scratch behind her ears.

"Hey, there, Harper," he murmured soothingly. "Keeping an eye on our best girl, are you?"

Shelby felt her cheeks flush at the affectionate nickname, a small smile forming at the corners of her mouth. "She's been my buddy through all of this," she said, reaching out to stroke Harper's soft fur. "She's a big help to me. She keeps me calm and centered."

As they settled into an easy rhythm, chopping

vegetables and seasoning the chicken, Shelby found herself opening up to Travis. She told him about her training with Fiona and Magill, about the way the magic seemed to flow through her veins like a living thing, and about the sense of purpose that had settled over her like a mantle.

Travis listened closely, trying to take it all in. "It's incredible," he said at last, his voice filled with awe. "This is beyond anything I could have imagined, but since I met you, there's been a lot I never could have imagined."

Shelby felt a flush of pleasure at his words, a warmth spreading through her chest that had nothing to do with the heat of the stove. "I just hope it will be enough," she said, her tone tinged with uncertainty. "The dark magic practitioners must be powerful, and we still don't know what the artifact is, or where to find it."

Travis reached out and took her hand, his fingers lacing with hers in a gesture of comfort and support. "We'll figure it out. We're getting close."

As they sat down to eat out on the covered porch, the conversation turned to the coordinates they had discovered on the gravestone, the cryptic clues that seemed to point to some location in the town.

"Wait until you see this." Travis's eyes lit up with

excitement as he pulled out a small map of Hamlet from his back pocket, spreading it out on the table between them.

"I think I know where it's leading us," he said, his finger tracing a path along the paper. "The old lighthouse, out near the cliffs. It's been abandoned for years, but there are stories about strange things happening out there, rumors of myths and magic."

Shelby felt a shiver of anticipation run down her spine at his words. "I know the old lighthouse. There are all kinds of rumors about it. I've heard there used to be a coven of witches that met there. When I was a kid, some people believed a serial killer lived there. I also heard that if two people kiss standing inside the lighthouse, they will marry one day. There are lots and lots of stories about the lighthouse. It sounds like that's where we need to go," she said. "First thing in the morning, we can head out there and see what we can find."

As the evening wore on and the candles burned low, Shelby and Travis were drawn closer together, the sparks of attraction that had always simmered between them flaring to life in the intimate glow of the apartment. They talked, laughed, and shared stories of their pasts.

When it was almost midnight, Travis got up to

leave, his hand lingering on Shelby's arm in a gentle caress.

"Get some rest," he murmured tenderly. "We have a big day ahead of us tomorrow."

Shelby nodded, her heart full to bursting with emotions she couldn't quite name. "Goodnight, Travis," she whispered, watching as he disappeared into the night, the ghost of his touch still lingering on her skin.

∼

The next morning dawned bright and clear with the sun shining over the streets of Hamlet as Shelby, Travis, and Harper set out toward the old lighthouse. The air was thick with the scent of salt and sea, the crashing of the waves against the cliffs a distant melody.

As they drove to the spot and parked along the side of the road, they walked along the sand and rocks to the old structure, its weathered stones and rusted iron rails standing stark against the blue of the sky. Shelby suddenly had the uneasy feeling that some unseen presence was tracking their movements.

Harper, too, seemed on edge, her fur standing on

end and her tail twitching with agitation. "Something's not right," she murmured as she glanced around. "We need to be careful."

Shelby and Travis exchanged a look, their hands instinctively reaching for each other as they climbed the narrow, winding stairs that led to the top of the lighthouse. The air grew colder as they ascended, the wind whipping at their hair and clothes with an almost supernatural fury.

At last, they reached the summit, the vast expanse of the ocean stretching out before them. Looking around inside the top of the lighthouse, they noticed something etched into the stone floor. It was another clue, another piece of the puzzle that would lead them to the artifact.

Travis knelt down to examine the faded markings of a compass rose. "It seems to be pointing back toward the old mill, the one by the river on the outskirts of town," he said at last, his voice filled with excitement. "Look here, there's a tiny image of the mill made with little stones, like a mosaic."

Shelby felt a thrill run through her at his words. "Then that's where we need to go," she said with a nod. "Could the artifact be there at the mill?" She reached for her rose quartz pendant. "I think my necklace will somehow help me know when we're near it."

"Let's go find out," Travis told her.

Harper let out a loud meow.

As they made their way back down the winding stairs, stepped outside, and walked toward the car with the old lighthouse looming behind them like a sentinel of the past, Shelby again had the unsettling sensation they were being watched. Her skin felt prickly, but she saw no one when her eyes searched the area.

The drive along the coast to the old mill was a quiet one, each of them lost in their own thoughts as they found a spot to park and then picked their way along the overgrown path that wound through the woods. The air was tinged with the scent of pine and earth, and the only sounds were the distant rushing of the river and the occasional cry of a bird overhead.

Approaching the crumbling mill, its weathered wooden walls and rusted water wheel standing silent and still in the dappled sunlight, Shelby felt a sudden chill run down her spine. She glanced up at the hill that rose above the mill, her eyes scanning the dense foliage for any movement.

And there, just for a moment, she saw him; a man, watching them from a trail in the shadows of the trees, his features obscured by the distance and the play of light and shadow. But there was something familiar about him, something that tugged at the edges of Shelby's mind.

When the sunlight suddenly changed, it hit her. The wide nose, the high cheekbones ... it was the same man who had tried to steal a book from her shop on the day of the big sale. The same man who had hurried away, leaving only questions and unease in his wake.

Shelby's heart began to race, her hand reaching out to grab Travis's arm. "Travis," she whispered with fear in her tone. "There's someone watching us. Up there on the hill. I think he was the one who tried to steal an antique book from my shop."

Travis's eyes narrowed, his body tensing as he followed Shelby's gaze, but the man was already gone, vanishing into the trees like a ghost. "We need to keep moving," he said, his voice low. "If he's one of the people after the artifact, we can't let him follow us."

With a nod, Shelby led the way toward the mill with Harper close at her heels. The interior was dark and musty, the air thick with the scent of seawater and old wood. Shafts of sunlight filtered through the broken windows, casting eerie patterns on the dust-covered floor.

"Look," Harper said suddenly. "Over there, in the corner."

Shelby turned to see a small, weathered wooden box the size of a mailbox tucked away in the shadows, its surface covered in strange symbols and markings.

"Could the artifact be inside that box?" With trembling hands, Shelby reached out and lifted the lid, her breath catching in her throat before she saw what lay inside. Her heart dropped in disappointment.

It wasn't the artifact but another clue, another piece of the puzzle that would lead them to it. At the bottom, three symbols were engraved into the wood ... a cryptic message that seemed to dance and shift before their eyes.

Travis leaned in closer, his eyes narrowed as he tried to make sense of the strange symbols. "It must be some kind of riddle," he said at last. "It's a clue that will take us to the next step on the journey."

Shelby took a photo of the symbols with her phone. "Let's try to work it out when we get home. I don't feel safe staying here any longer."

As they emerged from the mill, the sun was higher in the sky and the shadows were lengthening. Shelby took a quick look up to the trail where she'd seen the man staring down at them, and a cold shiver ran over her skin.

13

The sun had long since set over the town, but inside Shelby's cozy apartment, the light burned bright as she, Travis, and Harper studied the three cryptic symbols they'd discovered at the old mill. The living room held the scent of coffee and the sound of rustling papers as they worked to decipher the clues that would take them to the next step in their mission.

Shelby's apartment above the bookshop was a reflection of her warm personality. The walls were lined with bookshelves, each one filled to the brim with novels, histories, cookbooks, and biographies. Soft, comfortable furniture in shades of cream and blue invited visitors to sit and stay awhile, while potted plants and paintings of the sea added a touch of natural beauty to the space.

At the center of the room, a large, wooden table was strewn with notes, papers, and maps, as Shelby and Travis worked to unravel the next clue. The glow of the table lamp shone a warm light over their faces, illuminating the focus in their eyes.

"I feel like we're going in circles." Travis sighed, rubbing his eyes as he leaned back in his chair. "These symbols don't seem to match anything we've seen before."

Shelby nodded, her brow tight in concentration. "I know what you mean. How can we decode these symbols to show us where to go next?"

Harper, who had been quietly observing from her spot on the windowsill, suddenly jumped down and padded over to the table. "What about the mysterious book?" she asked. "Maybe there's something in there that could help us."

Shelby's eyes widened. "Harper, you're a genius," she said to the cat's mind, reaching for the old book that had started them on the journey. She turned to Travis. "Let's look for similar symbols in the book. I should have thought of this before."

Together, they began to carefully flip through the pages of the first section, their eyes scanning the faded text and intricate illustrations for any sign of the symbols they had found. Minutes turned into an hour, as they went over every inch of the images and translated text, their hopes rising and falling with each turn of the page.

"Wait a second," Travis said, his finger tracing a faint line of text on the first page that had been translated into English. "This passage here, it mentions something about 'the key to unlocking the past.' Could that be a reference to the symbols we found?"

Shelby leaned in closer, her heart racing with hope that they'd find something soon. "It's possible. Keep reading. See if there's anything else that stands out."

As Travis turned the page to one that hadn't yet been translated, Harper touched it with her paw. "Look," she spoke to Shelby's mind, pointing to a small illustration in the corner. "That symbol, it looks like one we found at the mill."

Shelby's eyes widened as she saw the unmistakable match. "Look here," she told Travis, her voice trembling with excitement. "Here's one of the symbols we found at the mill. But what does it mean?"

As if in answer to her question, the symbols on

the page began to glow, a soft, pulsing light that seemed to emanate from the heart of the book. Slowly, the strange markings began to shift and change, morphing into words and images that they could understand. The three symbols they'd found at the mill coalesced into an image of a road on the outskirts of Hamlet.

"The Harris Estate," Shelby said, her voice filled with wonder. "That's where we need to go next."

A flicker of recognition passed over Travis's face. "The Harris Estate is the place with the ghost story, the one about the tormented young woman who haunts the halls. Her name is Prudence Harris, right?"

Shelby nodded, her mind recalling the details of the legend. "Yes, that's right. She was born in Salem around 1676 and narrowly escaped the Witch Trials when she was just seventeen. Her father arranged for her to go to Virginia to live with relatives, but she never made it. She disappeared somewhere along the way, and her parents spent the rest of their lives searching for her, never knowing what had become of their beloved daughter."

Harper shivered, her fur standing on end. She communicated with Shelby, "And now her restless

Myths and Magic

spirit is said to haunt the estate, searching for the home and family she lost."

"It's such a tragic tale," Shelby said, her heart aching for the young woman who had been torn from everything she knew and loved. "I can't even imagine what she must have gone through, being sent away like that, never knowing if she would see her parents again."

Travis reached out and took Shelby's hand, his touch offering warmth in the midst of the sorrow and mystery that surrounded them.

He said, "There are events at the Harris Estate almost every week, and the place is open to the public for tours nearly every day. Why don't we go tomorrow evening? We can wander around and try to find the next clue."

Suddenly, Shelby's jaw dropped. "Oh, my gosh. I forgot something important. I've only been paying attention to finding the artifact. What do I do with it once we find it?"

The question began to pick at Shelby's mind. They couldn't just leave it out in the open, not with evil-doers in search of it. They had to have a plan to hide it right away.

Her voice was soft but urgent when she said, "We need to start thinking about where we're going to hide the artifact once we find it. Should the hiding place be inside somewhere? Should it be somewhere out in nature? I assume it has to remain in Hamlet. We can't take it out of the town."

Travis and Shelby exchanged a glance, their expressions growing serious.

"You're right," he said, his face thoughtful. "We've been focused on only half the task. We need to find a place that's safe, somewhere that only we know about."

Shelby's face turned slightly pale. "Since we'll know where it's hidden, what would stop the evildoers from torturing us to reveal its location?"

Travis remained silent for a few moments. "Let's complete the task, then we'll worry about our safety."

"Okay. Right. Now's not the time to be concerned about ourselves." Shelby took a deep breath and pushed her hair back from her face, still looking worried.

Harper's tail twitched, her eyes bright with an idea. "What about hiding the artifact in the bookshop?"

Shelby shared the suggestion with Travis. "The bookshop is a secure location that's been here for almost a century, and Magill could help me put up an extra protection spell to keep it safe."

Travis nodded. "Once we find it, we'll need to be careful moving it, though. We can't let anyone see us or suspect what we're doing."

"Maybe we could do it late at night," Shelby suggested, "after the shop is closed and the streets are quiet."

Harper purred, her eyes glinting with approval. "It could work, but we have to consider other hiding places, too. We have to make the right decision."

As plans began to take shape, Shelby felt a sense of relief wash over her.

"All right, team," she said, a grin spreading across her face. "Let's get some rest. We all have to be up bright and early tomorrow for work."

"I haven't heard a better idea all night. I'm worn out," Travis told her. "I'm ready to crawl into my bed." He patted the cat before standing up.

Shelby walked the detective to the door. "I know all of this is incredibly strange and crazy, and sometimes, I can't even believe what I'm involved with. Thanks so much for helping me."

"Well, if I wasn't helping out, my life would be pretty boring," Travis kidded. "Get a good night's sleep. We'll need our wits about us to do what we need to do."

They bid each other goodnight, and Shelby and the cat headed off to bed.

Resting her head against her pillow, the young woman was filled with a sense of awe at the amazing journey they were on. Only several months ago, she was quietly running her bookshop, and then her life had been forever changed as she was pulled into a realm of magic she had no idea existed.

As incredible as it sounded, she was the guardian of the artifact and the protector of the magic that flowed through the town she loved. Despite the confusion, fear, and disbelief about what she could do now, she knew that she was exactly where she was meant to be.

14

The first light of dawn was just beginning to peek through the curtains of Shelby's cozy apartment when a soft knock at the door roused her from her slumber. Rubbing the sleep from her eyes, she padded across the room, her bare feet sinking into the plush area rug as she made her way to the entrance.

Opening the door, she was greeted by Lucy holding a tray of freshly-baked maple and cinnamon buns, their sweet aroma filling the air and making Shelby's mouth water.

"Good morning, sunshine!" Lucy chirped, her blue eyes sparkling with warmth and affection. "I thought you could use a little pick-me-up before we start the day."

Shelby stepped aside to let her friend come inside. "Lucy, you're an angel. Those smell absolutely delicious. I'm sorry, I overslept. I was so tired."

"Then it's a good thing I showed up or you wouldn't have opened the bookshop until noon." Lucy came in and greeted Harper, then said to her friend, "Go take a shower and get dressed while I make the coffee."

Shelby returned fifteen minutes later as Lucy was setting the table with white mugs and small plates. The two women settled at the small, round kitchen table with steaming mugs of coffee and the sweet pastries. Harper, drawn by the enticing scent, leapt up onto a nearby chair, her eyes fixed on the treat-laden plate.

As they savored the sweet, sticky buns, Lucy began to tell Shelby about the new recipes she had been putting together at the bed and breakfast where she worked as the pastry chef.

"I've been experimenting with some healthier options," she explained, her voice filled with excitement. "I'm trying to create pastries that have no added sugar and no artificial sweeteners, but still taste amazing. I'm using different fruits, honey, and sometimes a bit of maple syrup in the recipes to give the new pastries a bit of a sweet taste. It's been a challenge, but I think I'm really onto a few things."

Shelby nodded, impressed by her friend's creativity and dedication. "If these maple-cinnamon sticky buns are any indication, I'd say you're definitely on the right track. They're absolutely delicious."

Lucy beamed, her cheeks flushing with pride. "Thanks. That means a lot. I'm so glad you like them."

As they continued to chat, Lucy's expression grew slightly dreamy, a soft smile playing at the corners of her mouth. "I have to tell you about the amazing dinner Ross and I had in Sweet Cove the other night. Being in a different place, just the two of us, seemed to make everything feel so romantic."

Shelby leaned in, her eyes wide with interest. "I want to hear all about it."

Lucy sighed, her gaze distant as she remembered the magical evening. "It was perfect. The restaurant was right on the water with these huge windows that looked out over the ocean. And Ross, he was so attentive and sweet. He even bought me a rose when we were walking around the main street afterwards."

Shelby squeezed her friend's hand, her heart full of happiness for her. "I'm so glad, Lucy. You and

Ross, you're perfect together. It sounds like things are really moving in the right direction."

Lucy nodded, her smile growing wider. "I think they are. I really do. We've been together for years and years, and sometimes, I think we take each other for granted. We sort of reignited our feelings for one another and remembered why we fell for each other in the first place."

As they discussed Lucy and Ross's romance, the weight of the previous day's events hung heavy in the air. Shelby couldn't keep her friend in the dark, not when the stakes were so high and the dangers so real.

Taking a deep breath, she began to recount the tale of her and Travis's search for the artifact, the clues they had uncovered, and how someone seemed to be watching their every move. Lucy listened intently, her expression filled with concern as Shelby described their trip to the lighthouse and the old mill, and the revelation of the next clue hidden within the mysterious book.

Shelby said, "The next clue is leading us to the Harris Estate. I know it's a lot to ask, but would you come with us? With your keen eye and your quick thinking, we could really use your skills on this one."

Lucy was silent for a moment, her eyes searching

Shelby's face as she weighed the risks and rewards of joining the quest. Finally, she said, "I'm worried about you. I'm afraid we'll be caught by the bad guys. What if they try to hurt you so they can take the artifact for themselves?"

Shelby stared at her friend. "I won't lie to you. The dangers are real, and I can't promise that everything will be okay, but I truly believe that they won't try to capture us just yet. They need us to lead them to the artifact's location, and they don't know which clue will be the one that reveals its hiding place."

She sighed, her gaze growing distant as she contemplated what was ahead. "Once we find it, that's when the real trouble will start. They'll likely attack when we have the artifact in our possession; try to steal it before we can hide it away. Until then, I think we're relatively safe, as long as we stay vigilant and stick together."

Lucy asked, "Is that supposed to make me feel better?"

"For the short term, yes." Shelby shrugged. "I don't think we'll be in danger at the Harris Estate because we're going there looking only for the next clue. If you don't want to come with us anymore, I certainly understand. In fact, maybe you should sit out this whole mess. If anything happened to you, I'd never forgive myself."

"And if anything happened to you because I wasn't with you, I'd never forgive *myself*," Lucy pointed out. "I'm with you, no matter what. But promise me one thing?"

Shelby tilted her head, her eyes questioning. "What's that?"

Lucy took a deep breath, her voice trembling slightly as she spoke. "Promise me that if things get too dangerous, if it looks like we're in over our heads, we'll back off. We'll find another way, or we'll ask for help. I'm not going to lose you, Shelby. You're my best friend, and I want us to grow old together."

Shelby felt a lump rise in her throat, her heart swelling with love and gratitude for the amazing woman sitting across her. "I promise."

"Okay." Lucy smiled, her eyes glistening. "So, you're stuck with me and I'm stuck with you, and we'll keep each other safe."

Harper, who had been listening to the exchange with wise, knowing eyes, let out a soft trill of approval, her tail swishing back and forth with contentment.

As the morning sun climbed a little higher in the sky and the sweet scent of cinnamon and maple lingered in the air, Shelby, Lucy, and Harper set their sights on the Harris Estate, ready to unravel the next piece of the puzzle and move one step closer to their goal.

∼

As the rays of the setting sun filtered through the windows of the Spellbound Bookshop, Shelby enjoyed the quiet and comforting atmosphere of her store. The place was closed for the rest of the day, the usual bustle of customers and the soft murmur of conversations replaced by a peaceful stillness that enveloped her like a warm hug.

The shop was a cozy haven with its shelves of books, plush armchairs, and pretty antique lamps that cast warm light over the hardwood floors. The faint aroma of tea and coffee from the complimentary beverage and pastry counter drifted in the air, creating an inviting and comfortable feeling.

Despite the tranquility of her surroundings, Shelby's mind was far from at ease. As she absently straightened the displays and rearranged the tables of books, her thoughts kept slipping back to the artifact and the seemingly endless quest to find it.

"Are we ever going to find it, Harper?" She

sighed, her voice tinged with frustration. "And if we do, we'll have to hide it fast before the dark practitioners can attack us. Where should we put it? We talked about hiding it in here, but what if the building gets knocked down someday? It has to be in an accessible place so the next guardian can get to it."

Harper, who had been perched atop a nearby bookshelf, jumped down and padded over to Shelby. "If you bury it out in a field, that field could be developed one day," the cat mused, her tail swishing back and forth. "If you place it near the coast, erosion or higher water levels could prevent it from being found again. Although, would that be a bad thing? If it couldn't be accessed, then the evil-doers would never be able to use it for dark purposes."

Shelby paused, considering Harper's words as she absently ran her fingers along the spines of the new releases. "I thought of that, too," she admitted, her face pinched in thought. "But Magill told me the artifact helps preserve and enhance the abilities of the Magicals who reside in town. Without the energy of the artifact nearby, our powers would lessen – they might even disappear. The artifact's power uplifts every magical being in Hamlet whose energy then joins together and amplifies everyone's skills and abilities."

As she spoke, Shelby noticed that Harper seemed distracted, her ears twitching as if she were listening to something far away.

"Did you hear what I said?" Shelby asked with concern.

Harper blinked, her eyes refocusing on Shelby. "Sorry. Yes, I did hear you. Our resident ghost is speaking to me."

Shelby's heart skipped a beat, her eyes widening with surprise. "Emily's here?" she asked, her voice barely above a whisper.

The cat tilted her head to the side for a moment, her expression one of deep concentration. "Emily says that you are close to finding the artifact," Harper relayed, her voice taking on an ethereal quality. "She warns that you must be vigilant. The people looking for the artifact will do anything to possess it, even kill."

Shelby felt a wave of dizziness wash over her, and she gripped the corner of the table for support. The weight of Emily's words settled over her like a physical burden, the gravity of the situation hitting her with full force. She knew there could be mortal danger, but hearing the words spoken hit her like a sledgehammer.

"Does she say anything else?" Shelby asked, her voice trembling slightly.

Harper's eyes clouded with confusion. "She says to find the tunnel."

Shelby's heart raced, her mind spinning. "What tunnel? Where is it?"

Harper merely shook her head, her expression apologetic. "Emily is gone."

A heavy silence settled over the bookshop, the only sound the soft ticking of the antique clock on the wall. Shelby's mind raced with questions, her thoughts tumbling over one another in a dizzying array.

What did Emily mean by a tunnel? Was it a literal tunnel, or some kind of metaphorical passage? How were they supposed to find it when they didn't even know where to begin looking?

As if sensing her distress, Harper leapt up onto the table, rubbing her head against Shelby's hand in a gesture of comfort. "We'll figure it out," she purred, her voice soft and reassuring. "We always do."

Shelby managed a small smile, drawing strength from her feline companion. "I really hope so," she said, taking a deep breath to steady herself. "We can't give up now, not when we're so close."

She glanced around the bookshop, her gaze lingering on the seemingly endless volumes that lined the shelves, each one holding its own stories and mysteries.

"We need to start looking for clues to find this tunnel," Shelby said, her voice growing stronger with each word. "Maybe there's something in the town's history, or in the old maps and documents we've been studying. We can't leave any stone unturned."

Harper nodded with determination. "We should talk to Magill and Fiona, too. They might have some insights or knowledge that could help us."

Shelby felt a flicker of hope in her heart, a spark of determination that burned bright and fierce. She knew the dark practitioners would stop at nothing to claim the artifact for their own, but she had hope they could stop them.

As the last traces of daylight faded from the sky and the shadows lengthened across the bookshop floor, Shelby glanced around the store.

Now along with locating the artifact, we have to find a mysterious tunnel.

A thought popped into her head. Could somewhere within these walls lay the key to ensuring the artifact's safety for generations to come?

15

In the early evening sunlight, Shelby, Lucy, Travis, and Harper walked to the outskirts of town and approached the imposing iron gates of the Harris Estate. The sprawling mansion with its graceful columns and peaked roofs, stood proudly amidst the meticulously manicured grounds, evidence of the wealth and refinement of the family who had called it home so long ago.

The estate was a sight to behold, with its lush gardens filled with fragrant blooms and towering oak trees that cast dappled shadows across the emerald lawn. A grand fountain, depicting a scene from Greek mythology, stood at the center of the circular drive, its cascading waters sparkling in the early evening light.

As they made their way up the gravel path, Shelby felt a sense of wonder at the sheer beauty of the place. "It's like something out of a fairy tale," she breathed, her eyes wide with amazement. "No matter how many times I come here, it never fails to impress. I can't believe people actually lived here, surrounded by all this grandeur."

Lucy nodded. "It's hard to imagine the kind of life they must have led," she agreed, her voice soft and wistful. "The parties, the social gatherings, the sheer opulence of it all."

Travis, ever the pragmatist, brought them back to the task at hand. "It's also hard to believe that such a magnificent home and refined family could have been touched by the shadow of witch accusations," he reminded them, with a sense of gravity in his tone. "The Harris family may have had wealth and status, but they weren't immune to the fear and paranoia of their time."

"You're certainly right about that. Shall we go in?" Shelby asked.

"No time like the present," Travis said.

Lucy glanced around the property. "If we don't find any clues while we're on the tour, we can wander around the grounds to see if there's anything here to guide us."

Shelby looked at Harper. "Stay nearby. Don't wander off. We won't be inside long."

Harper, ever the wise and cautious companion, agreed to wait for them outside, her keen feline senses alert for any sign of danger. With a final, reassuring nod to her friends, she settled herself on the branch of a nearby tree, her eyes scanning the grounds for any hint of trouble.

Despite having toured the mansion many times before, Shelby, Lucy, and Travis decided to take the historical tour once more, hoping to uncover a clue that might be hidden within the mansion. As they stepped through the grand entrance of the historic home, with its soaring ceilings and gleaming marble floors, they were immediately transported back in time to an era of elegance and wealth.

The tour guide, a distinguished older gentleman with a rich, melodic voice, led them through the various rooms, regaling them with tales of the Harris family's triumphs and tragedies. They marveled at the ornate furnishings and priceless works of art that adorned the walls, each one a symbol of the family's wealth and status.

As they entered the grand ballroom with its glittering chandeliers and polished parquet floors,

Shelby could almost hear the echoes of music and laughter from long-ago parties.

"Can you imagine dancing in this room?" she asked. "Wearing a beautiful gown, waltzing across the floor with a handsome suitor?"

Lucy giggled, her cheeks flushing pink at the thought. "It would be like something out of a romance novel," she agreed, her eyes sparkling. "Although, I don't know if I could handle wearing a corset and all those layers of petticoats."

Travis chuckled, shaking his head in amusement. "I think I'll stick to my modern-day suit and tie, thank you very much."

As they made their way up the grand staircase, Shelby's eyes were drawn to an oil painting that hung in the upstairs hallway. It depicted a teenage girl with delicate features and intelligent dark eyes, her porcelain skin seeming to glow in the soft light of the chandelier.

Shelby had seen the portrait before on other tours she'd taken. She studied the image, titled "Prudence," and felt an inexplicable sadness wash over her as she gazed at the long-deceased young woman in her formal gown, standing with a solemn expression. The image of the teen made Shelby think of the life Prudence might have known as an adult, had she not been accused of witchcraft.

"She looks so young," Shelby murmured, her voice filled with empathy. "To have her whole life ahead of her, only to be torn away from everything she knew and loved."

Lucy placed a comforting hand on Shelby's shoulder. "It's a tragedy," she agreed, her voice thick with emotion. "To think of all the lives destroyed by fear and ignorance."

The tour guide cleared his throat, recapturing the group's attention. "And here we have the Harris's only daughter, Prudence," he intoned, his voice tinged with a hint of melancholy. "Though not confirmed, many believe her tormented spirit roams these halls, searching for her parents and the life she was denied."

As the guide continued his tale, Shelby found herself transfixed by the painting, unable to tear her gaze away from Prudence's haunting eyes, and then, to her amazement, she saw the ghost's lips move slightly, and heard a soft, ethereal voice speak to her from beyond the grave.

"Look for what you seek in a dark place," Prudence whispered, her words echoing in Shelby's mind. "Where stones created something useful."

Shelby's heart raced, her palms growing clammy with excitement and fear. She strained to hear more, but Prudence's voice was fading, growing more distant with each passing second.

"Find the tunnel," the spirit murmured, her final words were a barely audible whisper. "For safekeeping."

Shelby felt a wave of dizziness wash over her, and she reached out to steady herself against the wall. Lucy and Travis, sensing her distress, were at her side in an instant, their faces etched with concern.

"Shelby, are you all right?" Lucy's eyes moved over her friend's face. "What happened?"

Shelby shook her head, trying to clear the fog that seemed to have settled over her mind. "I ... I heard her," she whispered, her voice trembling. "Prudence. She spoke to me from the painting."

Travis's eyes widened, his face filled with confusion. "What did she say to you?" he asked, his voice barely above a whisper.

"She gave me clues," Shelby replied, her heart still pounding. "Something about a dark place where stones created something useful. And a tunnel, for safekeeping."

Lucy and Travis exchanged a glance. They knew whatever message Prudence had imparted, it was sure to lead them one step closer to the artifact they sought.

Shelby pressed her fingers to her aching temple. "I'll tell you more once we're outside."

As the tour came to an end and they made their way back out into the evening light, Shelby's mind was reeling from what she had just experienced. She knew they needed to decipher Prudence's cryptic clues and do it fast before the dark practitioners could beat them to the punch.

Harper, sensing their agitation, climbed down the tree and trotted over to meet them, her expression full of curiosity. "What happened in there?" she asked, her tail swishing back and forth with anticipation. "Did you find any clues?"

Shelby nodded, a serious look on her face. "I heard Prudence speak to me. I hope I didn't imagine her words. We have to talk it over, but I need to sit down for a few minutes. Then we can try to make sense of what Prudence was trying to tell us."

Together, the four friends made their way to the nearby refreshment building, a charming cottage-like structure with a thatched roof and flower boxes overflowing with colorful blooms. Inside, the air was filled with the rich aroma of freshly brewed coffee and the sweet scent of baked goods.

As they settled themselves with beverages and sweets at a small table overlooking the gardens, Shelby recounted her experience with Prudence's ghost, her voice sounding urgent. Lucy, Harper, and Travis listened intently, their expressions growing more serious with each passing moment.

"A dark place where stones created something useful," Lucy mused, her eyes narrowed in thought. "Could she be referring to a basement or a cellar? Somewhere where stones were used to build the foundation?"

Travis shook his head, his eyes distant as he tried to piece together the clues. "I'm not sure," he said slowly, his voice tinged with uncertainty. "The way she phrased it, it sounds like the stones themselves were used to create something, not just as building materials."

Shelby nodded. "And the tunnel," she added. "She said it was for safekeeping. Could that be where the artifact is hidden?"

Harper's ears perked up, her whiskers twitching with excitement. "It's possible," she said to Shelby's mind, her voice low and thoughtful. "But Emily told you to look for a tunnel, too. A tunnel would be the perfect place to hide something valuable, especially if it's well-hidden and difficult to access. Maybe you're supposed to hide the artifact in a tunnel."

Even as they planned and plotted, Shelby had a prickly feeling that some unseen person was tracking their movements. She glanced around the garden, her eyes scanning the shadows for any hint of danger.

And then, just for a moment, she thought she saw a figure lurking behind a nearby hedge, a dark silhouette that seemed to vanish as quickly as it had appeared. With her heart racing, she turned to her friends, her eyes full of concern.

"We need to be careful," she whispered, her eyes wide with fear. "I have the sense someone's watching us, maybe even following us."

Travis's jaw clenched, his hand instinctively touching the concealed weapon he carried at his side. "We'll be ready for them," he said, his voice hard and determined. "Whoever they are, we won't let them get to the artifact before we do."

Lucy and Harper nodded. They knew the stakes were higher than ever, that the fate of all the Magicals who called Hamlet home hung in the balance.

As the sun moved closer to the horizon and the

shadows lengthened across the garden, Shelby and her friends discussed ways to unravel the mysteries and protect the magic that flowed through their beloved town.

16

The community center buzzed with energy as Shelby and Lucy made their way to the familiar classroom where the drum circle was held. The air was filled with the gentle murmur of conversation and the soft rustling of drums being set up, a prelude to the night's musical adventure.

As they entered the room, Lena Winthrop, the circle leader, greeted them with a warm smile and a friendly wave. "Welcome back, you two," she called out, her auburn hair shining in the soft light. "I'm so glad you could join us again."

Shelby and Lucy grinned, feeling instantly at ease in the welcoming atmosphere. They quickly chose their drums and found their spots in the circle, settling in among the other participants who were becoming familiar faces.

As the session began, Lena guided them through a series of warm-up rhythms, the room filling with the rich, pulsing sound of the drums. Shelby closed her eyes, letting the music wash over her, feeling the stress and worries of the day melt away with each beat.

Lucy, too, seemed lost in the moment, her hands moving deftly over the surface of her djembe, a look of pure joy on her face. The two friends exchanged a glance, their smiles wide and their eyes sparkling with the shared experience.

As the evening wore on, the group experimented with different rhythms and patterns, their laughter and encouragement mingling with the music. Shelby found herself lost in the flow, her hands seeming to move of their own accord, the drum almost becoming an extension of herself.

When the final beat faded away, the room erupted in applause and cheers, the participants reveling in the sense of unity and accomplishment they had achieved together. Lena beamed with pride, her eyes shining with the knowledge that she had helped create something truly special.

As the group made their way to the refreshment

table, chatting and laughing with one another, Lena approached Shelby, a curious expression on her face.

"You know, Shelby," she said, her voice thoughtful, "you have an incredible sense of rhythm. Have you played before?"

Shelby shook her head, the corners of her mouth turning up. "No, never, but something about it just feels right. I really enjoy the circle."

Lena nodded, her gaze studying Shelby's face. "I couldn't help but notice, though," she continued, her voice growing more serious, "there seems to be something bothering you. Your energy feels a little off, like there's a weight on your shoulders."

Shelby's eyes widened, surprised by Lena's perceptiveness. "Why do you think something's bothering me?" she asked, trying to keep her tone light and casual.

Lena shrugged, a knowing smile on her face. "Call it intuition, or maybe just a feeling, but if you ever need someone to talk to, I'm here. Sometimes it helps to share our burdens with others."

Shelby nodded, touched by Lena's concern. "Thank you. I appreciate that."

As they moved to mingle with the other participants, Shelby was drawn into a conversation with a young woman she hadn't seen before. The woman introduced herself as Penny Smith, a recent transplant to Hamlet who was trying to meet new people and get involved in the community.

"I thought taking some classes at the community center would be a good way to get to know people," Penny explained, her dark eyes sparkling with enthusiasm. "And I have to say, this drum circle has been one of the best decisions I've made so far."

Shelby grinned, feeling an instant kinship with the friendly, outgoing woman. "I know exactly what you mean," she said, nodding in agreement. "There's something about playing the rhythms together that seems to bring people closer together, don't you think?"

Penny nodded, her smile widening. "Absolutely. It's like we're all connected, even if we come from different backgrounds and have different stories. The drums are a great equalizer."

As they continued to chat, Shelby wondered if Penny might be a Magical, like herself. There was something about the woman's energy, a certain sparkle in her eye, that hinted at a deeper connection to the world around her.

But Shelby knew better than to broach the

subject directly. The existence of Magicals could be a controversial subject to bring up. Some people would be open and interested, and others would think you were crazy. It was a topic better discussed with those who shared the gift. Instead, she focused on getting to know Penny as a person, learning about her interests, her family, and what she did for work.

As the evening began to wind down and the participants started to say their goodbyes, Penny asked Shelby for her contact information, promising to stay in touch and perhaps even meet up for coffee sometime soon.

Lucy, who had been chatting with another group of drummers, made her way over to Shelby, a contented smile on her face. "Ready to head out?" she asked, her voice still buzzing with the energy of the night.

Shelby nodded. "Definitely. Let's walk back to my place."

As they stepped out into the humid night air, the stars twinkling overhead, Shelby and Lucy fell into an easy conversation.

"I can't get over how much I love these drum circles," Lucy gushed, her face glowing with happiness. "It's like, for a couple of hours every week, all the stress and worry just melts away, and I'm completely lost in the moment."

Shelby nodded, feeling the same sense of peace and contentment. "It's amazing, isn't it? And the people, too. Everyone is so open and friendly like we're all part of a welcoming community."

Lucy grinned, linking her arm with Shelby's as they walked. "Speaking of community, what did you think of Penny? She seems really cool and very nice."

Shelby's smile widened, her mind drifting back to the engaging conversation she had shared with the newcomer. "I liked her a lot. She's a math teacher. She accepted a job at the middle school and starts in late August. There's something about her, a kind of energy that just draws you in. I wouldn't be surprised if she turns out to be a Magical, too."

Lucy's eyes sparkled with intrigue. "Ooh, that would be exciting."

The two young women settled onto the plush sofa in Shelby's cozy apartment. Steam curled up from their mugs, filling the air with the soothing scent of chamomile and honey.

"I'm so glad you talked me into going to the drum

circle," Shelby said, a smile playing on her lips. "It's really fun. Somehow, it's both invigorating and calming at the same time. And it's nice to meet people we probably wouldn't have otherwise."

Lucy nodded, her blonde hair catching the soft light of the lamp. "Speaking of meeting new people, we should get together with Penny someday. She told me she likes hiking. We could show her some of the trails in the state park."

"Great idea," Shelby agreed, her eyes sparkling with enthusiasm. "It would be a perfect way to get to know her better and share some of our favorite spots."

As the conversation lulled, Shelby's thoughts drifted back to the events at the Harris Estate, a slight frown creasing her brow. "I've been thinking about the hints Prudence gave me when we were at the Harris Estate. I don't know how we're going to find the stones or the tunnel she mentioned," she mused, her voice tinged with worry. "I've been thinking that 'the stones that are useful' could mean stonewalls. There are miles of stonewalls around here. How would we know which one holds the clue?"

Lucy's gaze drifted over to Harper, who had been lounging on the armchair, her ears perked up as she listened to the discussion. "Maybe Harper can find it?" she suggested, her voice hopeful.

Shelby glanced at the cat, but Harper seemed lost in her own thoughts. Her eyes looked distant and unfocused.

"Did you hear what Lucy said?" she asked, trying to draw the feline's attention.

Harper remained silent for a few moments, her tail twitching slightly. When she finally spoke to Shelby's mind, her voice was soft. "Emily is here. She has something to say to me."

Shelby's eyes widened, and she scanned the room, hoping to catch a glimpse of the ghostly presence. She searched for any sign of the supernatural – a shimmering in the air, a small glowing orb, or even a faint sparkle – but the room remained unchanged, the only movement coming from the gentle flickering of the jar candles on the coffee table.

"What is she saying?" Shelby asked with anticipation.

Harper held up a paw, silencing the young woman for a moment as she listened closely to the unseen spirit. After a few seconds, she turned her attention back to Shelby, her expression serious. "She told me we all need to go down to the bookshop."

A wave of worry washed over Shelby's face, and she jumped to her feet, her tea nearly spilling from the mug. "Why? Is something wrong?" Her mind raced with possibilities, each more alarming than the last. "Is someone trying to break in?"

Lucy stood up, her own face etched with concern. "What's going on?"

Harper shook her head, her voice calm and reassuring. "I don't think that's it."

Shelby quickly explained to Lucy what Emily had told Harper, her words tumbling out in a rush of nervous energy.

Without hesitation, Harper padded toward the door that led to the staircase into the bookshop, her tail held high. "Come on," she urged, her voice filled with determination. "Let's go find out why she wants us downstairs."

The trio crept down the steps, the darkness of the bookshop enveloping them like a thick, velvety cloak. The familiar scent of books filled their nostrils, but the usual comfort it brought was overshadowed by a sense of unease.

"I don't hear anything," Shelby whispered as she moved cautiously through the shop, her eyes scanning for anything out of place. "Everything seems okay."

Harper, however, remained focused, her gaze fixed on a corner of the shop, her body still and alert.

Lucy sidled up to Shelby, her hand gripping her friend's arm, seeking comfort in the closeness. "What's Harper doing?" Lucy asked, her voice trembling slightly.

"I think Emily is talking to her," Shelby replied, her own heart pounding as she watched the cat's unwavering stare.

The seconds ticked by, each one feeling like an eternity as they waited for Harper to relay Emily's message. Finally, the cat's tail flicked, and she spoke, her voice filled with a quiet intensity. "Emily wants you to find the tunnel."

Shelby's eyes widened, her mind reeling from Harper's words. "Where is it?"

"What are you talking about?" Lucy questioned.

Shelby again relayed the information.

Harper blinked slowly, her gaze never leaving the corner of the shop. "It's in here somewhere."

A stunned silence fell over them, each of them trying to process the ghost's revelations. Shelby's mind raced, trying to recall any mention of a tunnel in the shop's history, but she drew a blank.

"In here? In the shop?" Lucy echoed, her voice

filled with a mix of disbelief and excitement. "Like, in the bookshop itself?"

Harper nodded, her eyes finally meeting Shelby's. "Emily says it's been here all along, hidden from view. She says it's the key to keeping the artifact safe."

Shelby's heart swelled with a sudden rush of hope and determination. If the tunnel was indeed within the walls of her beloved bookshop, then they may have found the perfect hiding place for the artifact.

"We need to start searching," Shelby declared. "Every nook and cranny, every shelf and floorboard. If there's a tunnel here, we'll find it."

Lucy and Harper nodded in agreement, their own faces set with determination.

They began to plan their search, dividing the shop into sections.

With a deep breath and a determined smile, Shelby turned to her friends, her eyes shining with the promise of discovery. "Let's get to work," she said, her voice filled with anticipation. "We have a tunnel to find."

17

The night was dark and still as Shelby, Harper, and Lucy stood in the quiet confines of the Spellbound Bookshop. The overhead lights were on, but the women also carried flashlights to better see any small thing that might lead them to a tunnel. The flickering beams of the flashlights cast eerie shadows on the tall bookshelves that surrounded them. The air was thick with the weight of the magic they needed to protect.

Shelby turned to her companions. "Okay, let's start searching for any sign of this tunnel. Emily said it's here, somewhere in the older part of the building. We need to look for anything out of the ordinary, any clue that might lead us to the entrance."

Lucy nodded, her hair glinting in the light. "Got

it. I'll start by checking behind the shelves along the walls. Maybe there's a hidden button or a secret panel we've never noticed before."

Harper, her keen feline senses on high alert, padded silently through the shop, her ears twitching at every creak and groan of the old floorboards. Her eyes, glowing green in the darkness, scanned the ceilings and corners, searching for any hint of an opening or a hidden mechanism.

As they moved methodically through the space, their flashlights sweeping over every inch of the shop, Shelby worried they wouldn't find anything. The building had stood on this spot for generations, once housing a general store and now a haven for book lovers. With the revelation of a secret tunnel hidden within its walls, it seemed that the shop held even more mysteries than she'd ever imagined.

Lucy, her eyes narrowed in concentration, paused before some particularly heavy wooden shelves, the surface worn smooth with age. "Hey, Shelby? Can you help me move these books? I want to see if there's anything behind them."

Shelby hurried over, and together, the two friends removed books from a few of the shelves, and then gripping the edges, they strained to move it. With a grunt of effort, they managed to shift it a few inches, revealing a small gap between the wall and the unit.

Lucy shined her flashlight into the darkness, and her eyes focused as she searched for any sign of a hidden entrance. "I don't see anything," she said, her tone tinged with disappointment. "Just a bunch of dust and cobwebs."

Shelby sighed, her shoulders sagging as they carefully maneuvered the shelf back into place and restocked the books. "Let's keep looking," she urged, trying to keep her spirits up. "The tunnel has to be here somewhere. We just need to keep at it."

As they continued their search, Lucy's voice broke the silence once more, a note of curiosity in her tone. "I was wondering ... who would put a tunnel under this building in the first place? I mean, it seems like an awful lot of work to keep something hidden."

Shelby paused. "Well, there were lots of tunnels and secret passages built during the time of the Underground Railroad," she explained, her voice taking on a distant quality. "They were used to help slaves escape to freedom, to hide them from their pursuers, and guide them along the way. There were networks of safe houses, secret routes, and tunnels to hide in or to use to get safely out of a building and into the woods, a field, or a quiet lane."

Lucy's eyes widened, a flicker of understanding dawning on her face. "Oh, right. I remember learning about that in history class. It's amazing to think that people went to such lengths to help others, even at great risk to themselves."

Shelby nodded. "It just goes to show the power of compassion and the human spirit. Even in the darkest of times, there are always those who will stand up for what's right, no matter the cost."

As they spoke, Harper trilled from the next room, her tail twitching with excitement. Shelby and Lucy hurried to see what she might have found.

"Do you see something, Harper?" Shelby asked, her heart leaping with anticipation.

The cat was staring into a corner where two shelves abutted one another. "Emily was standing here a moment ago. I think she was trying to tell me something."

Lucy hurried to the corner and moved her hands over the shelves. "Hold on. There's a latch here."

Shelby hurried to her friend's side while Lucy jiggled the latch.

"It won't budge," Lucy said. "Do you have any of

those spray cans of lubricant that handymen use to unstick something?"

"Oh, I know what you mean." Shelby ran out of the room and into the storeroom. In less than four minutes, she was back carrying a canister of WD-40. She craned her neck to see where the latch was, then sprayed some of the product onto it.

Lucy fiddled again with the latch. "I got it. I undid it." She looked at the shelves, and then her face lit up. "Look, if we push on this shelf, maybe it will slide over the other one."

The two women struggled and pushed against the old shelving, and on the last push, it began to move.

"Oh, my gosh, it's sliding."

Harper spoke to Shelby's mind. "A little more. There's something there. Come see."

When Shelby and Lucy stepped back to look, there was a short, narrow door in the wall.

"Look at that." Lucy gestured in amazement. "A tiny hidden door. I don't believe it."

Shelby moved slowly toward it. She reached out, her fingers trembling slightly as she pressed the rusty latch. With a deep breath, she leaned her shoulder into it, and the door squeaked as it swung open, revealing a narrow, winding staircase that descended into the darkness below. "There's a staircase. It's rickety. Be careful on it."

Lucy gasped, her hand flying to her mouth in shock. "Is that ... the tunnel? It's what Emily was talking about."

Shelby nodded, her eyes wide with wonder. "I think it is, but where does it lead? And why was it hidden away like this for so many years?"

Harper, her tail swishing back and forth, took a tentative step forward, her paws barely making a sound on the stone steps. "There's only one way to find out," she mewed to Shelby's mind, her voice filled with a quiet determination. "We have to follow it."

Shelby and Lucy exchanged a glance, their expressions mirroring the same nervous anticipation fluttering in their hearts. With a nod of silent agreement, they stepped forward, their flashlights cutting through the gloom as they began their descent into the unknown.

As they made their way down the narrow staircase, the air grew colder and more humid, the walls pressing in on them from all sides. The beam of Shelby's flashlight danced over the dirt, wood, and rough-hewn stone, revealing patches of moss and lichen that clung to the old masonry.

Lucy, her voice hushed, reached out to trail her fingers along the wall, marveling at the history that surrounded them. "Can you imagine the people who must have used this tunnel, all those years ago?" she whispered, her words echoing softly in the darkness. "The bravery it must have taken to risk everything for a chance at freedom?"

Shelby nodded, her heart swelling with respect for those who had come before. "It's humbling, isn't it? To think of the sacrifices they made, the dangers they faced, it puts our own struggles into perspective."

Harper, her keen senses guiding her through the gloom, paused a few yards from the staircase, her ears twitching as she listened for any sign of movement or danger. "The coast is clear," she reassured Shelby telepathically. "But we have to be careful. There's no telling what we might find down here."

"Should we follow it?" Shelby asked.

"What if it collapses?" Lucy warned. "It probably hasn't been used in almost two centuries." She checked her phone. "Amazingly, I have service."

"Okay, let's walk. If we get stuck in here, we can call for help."

With deep breaths, Shelby and Lucy stepped forward, their footsteps echoing softly on the packed earth of the tunnel floor. The passage was narrow and low in spots, forcing them to hunch their shoulders and duck their heads as they made their way forward.

They moved down the low-ceilinged tunnel with Harper leading the way. They stopped every few minutes to listen, and when they didn't hear anything, they went on.

Feeling nervous to be walking about in an old tunnel, Lucy held tightly to the back of Shelby's shirt, her short nervous breathing the only sound that could be heard.

As they walked, their flashlights sweeping over the rough-hewn walls and the gnarled roots that snaked across the ceiling, Shelby felt a strong connection to the past, to the countless souls who had walked this same path in search of freedom and hope.

Just as the tunnel began to feel like it might go on forever, they rounded a bend and found themselves emerging into the corner of a nearby small park located on a quiet road not far from the main street. The entrance into the tunnel was blocked by a huge boulder surrounded by weeds and small brush. They squeezed around the rock into the night and marveled at where they were in town.

Harper trilled as she padded over the soft grass.

"It's a twisty tunnel," Shelby observed. "I never would have guessed that it led here."

"What an adventure," Lucy exclaimed in delight now that they had successfully emerged from the scary place.

"There are two entrances to this tunnel, one here in the park and one from the bookshop," Shelby pointed out. "The tunnel would make a good hiding place for the artifact."

"If we ever find it," Lucy reminded her.

Shelby suggested, "Why don't we head back? We can look for a good spot to dig a hole in the tunnel's wall. That's where we'll hide the artifact."

The threesome took another look around the small park, then turned and headed back into the tunnel.

Now, if only they could find the secret artifact and keep it safe so the magic of the town could be preserved for generations to come.

～

The sun-dappled path leading to Magill's enchanting cottage was a welcome sight for Shelby as she made her way through the lush, green landscape. The air was filled with the sweet scent of blooming flowers and the gentle rustling of leaves in the warm breeze.

As she approached the cozy home, Shelby felt a sense of belonging, knowing that she was about to meet with two of her most trusted mentors and allies.

Fiona greeted her at the door, her warm smile and twinkling eyes a familiar and reassuring presence. Magill, seated in her favorite armchair by the fireplace, looked up as Shelby entered, her expression a mix of wisdom and concern.

"Welcome, my dear," Magill said. "Please, have a seat. We have much to discuss."

As Shelby settled into the plush sofa, Fiona took her place beside the young woman. The three sat in silence for a moment, before Shelby said, "I found the perfect place to hide the artifact."

She told the women about her, Harper, and Lucy's search last night for a tunnel that Emily the ghost wanted them to find. "It took us a while, but we finally found a small door in the bookshop that led down a steep staircase and into the tunnel."

Magill and Fiona asked questions and Shelby answered them, and then, Magill bestowed her blessings on the hiding place. "Well done. It seems the tunnel is the right choice."

A few moments later, Magill spoke again, her words heavy. "Shelby, we have consulted with powerful intuits and have tried to sort the information we've gathered into myths and facts. There is much we need to share with you about the artifact and the ancient magic it possesses."

Shelby leaned forward, her heart racing with anticipation and a hint of trepidation. "I'm ready to learn," she said, her voice steady and determined.

Magill nodded, her eyes distant as she delved into the depths of her knowledge. "You once asked me why the artifact can't be left where it is, why it must be moved. The reason is that both the powerful spell keeping the artifact's whereabouts secret, and the power within the artifact itself, eventually wear down and lose enough of their strength that some of those who wish to obtain it can sense its presence. Then they make their move to steal the artifact when the guardian has to relocate it."

Shelby absorbed the information, her mind racing. "That makes sense," she said. "When I hide it, how will I know the correct spell to use to protect it?"

A small, knowing smile played on Magill's lips. "The spell will come to you," she explained, her voice filled with quiet confidence. "You just have to be open to receiving the message."

Shelby nodded, a flicker of doubt creeping into her heart. "I hope I'm able to do what needs to be done," she confessed, her voice barely above a whisper.

Fiona gave her shoulder a gentle squeeze. "You are stronger than you know. The artifact chose you for a reason. As soon as you touch it, the artifact's full power will be restored. Trust in yourself and the magic that flows through you."

Magill cleared her throat, drawing their attention back to the matter at hand. "There is something else we have learned, something we initially thought might be a myth, but have discovered is, in fact, true. As soon as you hide the artifact, Shelby, the old book will disappear, but not before something else happens."

Shelby's eyes widened, her heart skipping a beat. "What do you mean? What else will happen?"

Magill's expression grew somber, her voice heavy with the weight of the revelation. "You and your friends, those who helped you search for and hide the artifact, will lose all memory of this adventure. It is a safeguard to ensure that the evil-doers cannot capture and torture you to reveal the artifact's location. This way, you will all be safe."

Shelby felt as though the ground had shifted beneath her feet, her world tilting on its axis. "Our memories will be wiped clean? But that shouldn't happen. We should be able to keep our memories of the artifact and our attempts to protect it."

Magill shook her head. "It won't be possible. This is the way it has worked for centuries, and it cannot be changed. It's to protect you and your friends."

Tears stung Shelby's eyes as she struggled to come to terms with the reality of the situation. "Who will wipe our memories?" she asked, her voice trembling with emotion.

Fiona spoke softly. "The magic of the artifact will do it. When you hide it, the spell will be cast, and your memories will fade like a dream upon waking."

Magill, her voice low and urgent, added, "When the artifact is in danger again, the old book will reappear, creating clues that will lead the next guardian to its location in the tunnel."

Shelby's heart raced, the weight of her responsibility bearing down on her like a physical force. Magill, sensing her distress, leaned forward, her eyes locked with Shelby's.

"Of course," she said, her tone serious and unwavering, "you have to survive this ordeal and protect the artifact first."

The cold truth of the adventure settled over Shelby like a suffocating blanket, making her feel weak and vulnerable, and the thought of losing her memories, of forgetting the incredible journey she had undertaken with her friends, nearly broke her heart.

As a tear slipped down her cheek, Shelby felt a deep, aching sadness that, if she succeeded in protecting the artifact, she would remember nothing of the adventure. The laughter, the tears, the moments of triumph and despair – all would be lost to the mists of time.

Fiona gathered Shelby into her arms, holding her close. Magill, her eyes filled with understanding, rose from her chair and joined them, her presence a comfort to Shelby's disappointment.

"We'll help you," Magill whispered. "We will practice spells and skills, and do everything in our power to ensure your success."

Shelby, drawing strength from the love and support of her mentors, nodded, her resolve hardening like steel. She knew she had no choice but to see it through.

She would protect the artifact, no matter the cost to herself.

As the three women sat together in Magill's cottage, they began to plan and prepare, their hearts heavy with the knowledge of what was to come, but their spirits buoyed by the power of the magic that flowed through them.

Shelby would do what was necessary to meet with success, even if it meant sacrificing her memories in the process.

18

The sun was high in the cloudless sky as Shelby and Lucy set out on their favorite hiking trail, the air filled with the sweet scent of pine and the gentle rustling of leaves in the warm breeze. Beside them, Penny Smith, the young woman they'd met at the drum circle, walked with an easy stride, her eyes full of curiosity.

Penny was a striking woman, with long, dark hair that cascaded down her back in loose waves and eyes the color of dark chocolate. She had an air of confidence about her, a sense of self-assurance that seemed to radiate out from her. As they walked, she told them about her recent move to Hamlet.

"I came from a small town in Colorado," she explained, her words painting a vivid picture of snow-capped mountains and winding trails. "It was beautiful there, but I felt like I needed a change, a new adventure. When I heard about the teaching position at the middle school, I knew I wanted to move here."

Lucy's eyes widened with interest, her face breaking into a warm smile. "Shelby told me you're a teacher," she said with admiration. "What subject do you teach?"

Penny grinned, her love for her chosen profession shining through in her words. "Math," she replied, her tone light and engaging. "I know it's not everyone's favorite subject, but I just love the way it challenges the mind and the way it reveals patterns and connections in the world around us."

As they made their way deeper into the woods, the trail winding through the lush, green landscape, for a moment, Shelby sensed something was off, a strange sensation that prickled at the back of her neck and set her nerves on edge. It was as if the air around them was charged with an unseen energy, a force she couldn't quite put her finger on. She glanced around to see if anyone was hiking nearby, but she saw no one.

"So, Penny," Lucy said, her tone bright and friendly as they walked, "what made you interested in Hamlet? It's not often we get new faces around here who aren't tourists."

Penny smiled, her eyes crinkling at the corners as she turned to look at Lucy. "Oh, you know how it is," she said. "I'm a bit of a nomad, always on the move. I like to experience new places and meet new people. Hamlet just seemed like the perfect place to stop for a while, to see what life has in store. And the coastline looked so beautiful in the pictures I saw on the Internet. It seems like a lovely small town."

Shelby felt a flicker of unease at Penny's words, a sense that there was more to the woman's story than she was letting on, but she pushed the feeling aside, telling herself that she was just being paranoid, that the stress of their quest for the artifact was making her see shadows where there were none.

"Well, we're glad to have you here," Shelby said, forcing a smile to her face. "Hamlet's a special place, filled with a lot of history and magic. I'm sure you'll find plenty of adventures to keep you busy."

Penny's eyes sparkled with interest at the mention of magic, a look of keen curiosity crossing her face. "Magic?" she asked, her voice low and intrigued.

Shelby caught herself. "Yeah, I mean it's a magical place, a pretty town with a lovely rocky coastline, a few small beaches, woods and trails, and nice people."

Penny laughed. "I thought you were referring to actual magic like in nearby Salem. I've always been drawn to the mystical, the unexplained. Anyway, I'd love to learn more about the town's history."

Lucy, ever the enthusiastic tour guide, launched into a detailed explanation of Hamlet's rich past, regaling Penny with tales of the town's founding and the mysterious events that had shaped its destiny over the centuries. "We're not exactly like Salem, but we have tales of witches, warlocks, and magic woven into the town's history."

As they walked and talked, the trail began to get steeper, the path growing narrower with each passing step. Shelby felt her sense of unease nagging at her. The strange energy she'd sensed earlier seemed to be growing more intense, more palpable with every twist and turn of the trail.

Then, just as they rounded a particularly sharp bend in the path, Shelby felt it – a sudden, overwhelming surge of power that seemed to crackle through the air like electricity. She stumbled, her hand reaching out to steady herself against a nearby tree trunk and her breath coming in short, sharp gasps.

"Shelby?" Lucy's voice was filled with concern as she hurried to her friend's side, her hand reaching out to offer support. "Are you all right? What's wrong?"

Shelby shook her head, trying to clear the fog that seemed to have settled over her mind. "I ... I don't know," she mumbled, her words slurring slightly as she struggled to regain her composure. "I just felt weird. It's hard to explain. I think it's a combination of low blood sugar and the heat."

Lucy pulled a granola bar from her backpack and handed it to her friend.

Penny, who had been walking a few paces ahead, turned back to look at Shelby, her expression full of worry. "Are you sure you're okay?" she asked. "Maybe we should take a break and sit down for a bit. We don't want you to overexert yourself."

But Shelby waved off their concern, pushing herself from the tree and forcing a smile to her face. "No, no, I'm fine," she insisted, her voice growing stronger with each word, even as the strange sensation continued to prickle at the back of her mind. "Just a little dizzy for a moment there. Let's keep going. I don't want to ruin our hike." She took a bite of the bar.

As they continued on their way, the strange

sensation that had overwhelmed Shelby began to fade, replaced by a growing sense of unease and suspicion. She had a feeling there was something off about Penny, something that didn't quite add up, despite the woman's friendly demeanor and engaging conversation.

And then, as they paused to take in the breath-taking view of the valley below, Penny spoke, her voice casual and offhand, almost dismissive in tone. "You know, I probably won't be in Hamlet for very long," she said, her eyes fixed on the horizon, her expression unreadable. "I never stay in one place for too long. It's just not my style. I like to keep moving, keep exploring. I guess I'm just a rolling stone."

Shelby felt a slight chill run down her spine at Penny's words. For a moment, she was gripped by a powerful urge to confront the woman, to demand answers to the questions that swirled in her mind, and to uncover the truth behind her mysterious arrival in Hamlet.

But as quickly as the feeling had come, it vanished, replaced by a sense of confusion and doubt. She scolded herself for being so paranoid. Was the stress of their quest making her see things that weren't really there? After all, Penny had been nothing but friendly and engaging throughout their hike, sharing stories of her travels and her love for teaching. Shelby felt guilty for being so suspicious.

Lucy, oblivious to Shelby's inner turmoil, chattered away happily, pointing out the different plants and animals they passed along the way. Her voice was filled with the joy and wonder of someone who truly loved the natural world.

Penny, too, seemed perfectly at ease. Her smile was warm and genuine as she listened to Lucy's explanations, asking questions and sharing her own knowledge of the flora and fauna around them.

As they made their way back down the trail, the sun beginning to dip toward the horizon and the shadows lengthening across the forest floor, Shelby still had a feeling that something was wrong, that some unseen danger lurked just beyond the edge of her perception. It was as if the air around them was charged with a strange energy, a force that she couldn't quite put her finger on. She looked around, but again, saw nothing out of place.

She glanced over at Penny, trying to read the woman's expression, to gauge her intentions, but Penny's face was a mask of calm. Her eyes were clear and unclouded as she walked along beside them, and her steps were sure and steady on the uneven terrain.

"Thank you so much for showing me this trail," Penny said as they emerged from the woods and back into the bright sunlight of the parking lot. "It was absolutely beautiful. I can see why you love it so much. The way the light filters through the trees, the sound of the birds singing in the branches ... it's like something out of a fairy tale."

Lucy beamed with pride, her cheeks flushed with exertion and happiness. "We're so glad you enjoyed it," she said, her voice warm and sincere. "We'll have to do this again sometime soon, maybe even make it a regular thing. It's always nice to have a new hiking buddy."

Shelby nodded, forcing a smile to her face even as her mind raced with doubts and questions. "Definitely," she agreed, her voice sounding hollow and false to her own ears. "It's always nice to share our favorite places with new people."

As they said their goodbyes and parted ways, Shelby sensed that some crucial piece of the puzzle was missing. She watched as Penny walked away toward her car, her long hair swaying in the breeze, and felt a shiver run down her spine, a sense of unease that she couldn't put into words.

Who was this woman, really? Shelby knew that she couldn't trust anyone, not fully, not until the artifact was safe and the dark forces that sought to claim it were defeated.

She would not let her guard down; would not let herself be swayed by false friends or empty promises. She had a mission, and she had to see it through to the end.

With a sigh, she regretted being so suspicious of new people ... being judgmental and unfriendly. Every new person she'd met or run into recently had made her feel distrustful and cynical — Evelyn Blackwell, the man who seemed to be trying to steal an antique book from her shop during the big sale, and now Penny.

As they drove back into town, the sun setting over the hills, Shelby couldn't wait for this task to be over, so she could stop looking over her shoulder with distrust and fear and return to being her normal self.

19

The light from the setting sun filtered through the windows of Shelby's cozy apartment, casting a soft, golden luster over the faces of Travis and Lucy as they sat together on the plush sofa with Harper squeezed between them. Shelby, her expression grave and her heart heavy with the weight of the knowledge she carried, paced before them, her footsteps muffled by the thick area carpet.

"There's something I need to tell you," she began, her voice low and somber. "It's something that Magill and Fiona recently revealed to me, about what will happen when we find the artifact and hide it away."

Travis and Lucy exchanged a glance, their eyes full of concern. They had seen the toll this quest had taken on their friend, the sleepless nights and the constant worry that haunted her every waking moment.

"What is it, Shelby?" Travis asked, his voice gentle. "Whatever it is, it'll be all right. You know we'll help any way we can."

Shelby took a deep breath, steeling herself for the words that she knew would change things. "When we hide the artifact," she said, her voice trembling slightly, "our memories of this entire adventure will be wiped clean. We won't remember anything about the book, the clues, the artifact itself, where we went, or what we did. It's a safeguard to protect us and the town from those who would use the artifact's power for evil."

For a moment, the room was silent, the only sound the soft ticking of the clock. Travis and Lucy stared at Shelby, their expressions a mix of shock and disbelief.

"Our memories ... wiped clean?" Lucy whispered, her voice barely audible. "But how? Why?"

Shelby sank down onto the chair across from them, her shoulders slumping with the weight of the information. "It's the way it's always been," she explained, her voice heavy with resignation. "The magic of the artifact will erase our memories to ensure that we can't be forced, or tortured, to reveal its location. It's the only way to keep it safe, and to protect us."

Travis, his jaw clenched with frustration, shook his head. "But that's not fair," he argued, his voice rising with each word. "We've risked quite a lot to find this artifact, to keep it out of the wrong hands. How can we just forget it all, like it never even happened?"

Shelby reached out, taking his hand in hers and squeezing it gently. "I know," she murmured. "Believe me, I had the same reaction when I heard what would happen. I don't want to forget any of this either. The things we've seen, the challenges we've faced ... they've brought us closer to together, but this is the way it has to be. The artifact is too powerful and too dangerous to risk falling into the wrong hands."

Lucy, her face pale and her eyes wide with a dawning understanding, spoke up, her voice soft but clear. "Shelby's right," she said, her gaze locked with Travis's. "We have to do this, for the town and everyone in it. Our memories of this ... they're a small price to pay for the safety and security of Hamlet."

Travis, his shoulders slumping in defeat, nodded

slowly. "I know," he admitted, his voice gruff with emotion. "It's just ... I don't want to forget this, forget what we've done together. The things we've been through, the bond we've formed ... it means a lot to me."

Shelby, her heart aching with the same sense of loss and grief, pulled them both into a tight hug, a few tears finally spilling over and falling down her cheeks. "We may forget the details," she whispered, her voice choked with emotion, "but the love and friendship we share, the connection we have ... that will never fade away. It's a part of us, now and forever."

As they held on to each other, drawing strength and comfort from the warmth of their embrace, Harper stood on the sofa beside them, her purr a soothing sound to their troubled hearts.

"It's time," the cat mewed softly to Shelby, her voice echoing in the young woman's mind. "The tunnel is waiting, and the artifact must be hidden away. We have to be brave, and trust in the magic that guides us."

"We need to get going." Shelby wiped at the tears on her cheeks.

With heavy sighs, Shelby, Travis, and Lucy made

their way down the narrow staircase that led to the bookshop below.

The shop was dark and silent, with the only light coming from the soft glow of the streetlamps that filtered through the windows. Harper led the way, her tail held high as she guided them to the secret door that concealed the entrance to the tunnel.

As they descended the worn stone steps, the air grew colder and damper, with the walls pressing in on them from all sides. Travis, carrying a heavy metal box clutched tightly in his hands, followed closely behind, his forehead lined with concentration.

"I wasn't sure how big of a box to get," he explained, his voice echoing softly in the darkness. "We don't know what the artifact looks like, or how much space it will need. I just hope it's big enough to keep it safe."

Shelby nodded in understanding. "We'll make it work," she assured him, her voice steady and strong. "I can't imagine it's very big. The smaller it is, the easier it will be to hide."

As they made their way deeper into the tunnel, the beam of Lucy's flashlight danced over the rough-hewn walls, showing the old stones and dirt. The air was thick with the scent of earth, and the only sound was the soft scuffing of their footsteps on the packed dirt floor.

Halfway through the passage, Shelby paused, her eyes scanning the walls for a spot that looked promising. "Here," she said at last. "This section looks like it's mostly dirt and wood, without any big rocks in the way. We can dig here and hide the box inside the hole in the wall."

Travis and Lucy nodded, their faces grim as they set to work, their trowels biting into the soft earth with a steady rhythm. They worked quickly and efficiently, taking care to pile the dirt into the bucket Shelby had brought, so as not to leave any trace of their presence.

When the hole was deep enough, Travis carefully pushed the metal box into the cavity, his hands shaking slightly with the weight of the moment. Shelby and Lucy helped him to cover it over with dirt, packing it tightly to ensure that it would remain hidden from prying eyes. Travis slipped a rock into the opening, concealing the box from view, but keeping it accessible for when the time came to place the artifact inside.

As they stepped back to admire their handiwork, a sudden sound from the darkness beyond made them freeze, their hearts leaping into their throats.

Harper, her ears twitching and her tail puffed up in alarm, crouched low to the ground, her eyes scanning the tunnel for any sign of danger.

"What was that?" Lucy whispered, her voice trembling with fear. "Did you hear it?"

Shelby, her own heart pounding with a sickening dread, nodded silently. Her hand reached out to grasp Travis's arm. They stood there, frozen in place, for what felt like an eternity, their ears straining for any hint of movement or threat.

And then, the sound they'd heard was replaced by the soft hooting of an owl somewhere in the distance. Shelby let out a shaky breath, her shoulders sagging with relief.

"It was just an owl," she murmured, her voice barely audible over the pounding of her own heart. "We're safe, but we need to keep moving and get out of here before anyone notices us leaving the tunnel."

With a nod of agreement, they set off, their footsteps quickening as they made their way toward the end of the tunnel. As they emerged into the small park beyond and the cool night air washed over them, Shelby had the uneasy feeling that some unseen presence was tracking them.

She glanced over her shoulder, her eyes scanning the shadows for any sign of pursuit, but the park was empty and still, the only sound the gentle rustling of the leaves in the breeze.

"We should split up," Travis suggested. "We'll each take different routes back to the bookshop, so no one sees us together. We can meet up again once we're sure the coast is clear."

Shelby and Lucy nodded, their faces looking grim. They quickly surveyed the area, looking for the best ways to exit the park and return to the safety of the bookshop without drawing attention to themselves.

"I'll take the path along the river," Lucy said, pointing to a narrow trail that wound its way through the trees. "It's a bit longer, but it's less likely that anyone will see me."

Travis nodded, his eyes scanning the surrounding streets. "I'll cut through the alleyways behind the main street," he said, his voice low and determined. "There are plenty of shadows and hiding spots, in case anyone is watching."

Shelby, her heart still racing from adrenaline, took a deep breath, her mind already mapping out her own route. "I'll circle around the park and come in from the other side of town," she said, her voice steady and calm. "We'll meet back at the bookshop in thirty minutes, once we're sure it's safe."

With a final nod of agreement, they set off into the night, each taking a different path through the sleepy streets of Hamlet. As Shelby walked, her senses became heightened and alert for any sign of danger.

As she and Harper made their way back to the safety of the bookshop, she felt a sense of amazement at the incredible journey they had undertaken. From the moment the mysterious book had appeared in her life, she had been set on a path that had led her to this moment of danger and discovery. She knew the dark forces that sought to claim the artifact for their own would stop at nothing to see their twisted dreams realized. But she also knew her magic and her friends would guide her through whatever storm lay ahead.

As the stars twinkled overhead, relief washed over her when she saw Lucy emerging from the trees behind the main street, and as she got closer to her shop, she saw a tiny light in the window and knew Travis was safe inside.

She couldn't wait for this adventure to be over, to know they were all unscathed and the magic of their hometown was safe and sound once more.

20

It was late the next night, and the Spellbound Bookshop was quiet and still as Shelby and Harper moved from shelf to shelf, re-arranging some of the books in the glow of the lamps. Beyond the shop's windows, some tourists walked back to their hotels from the pubs.

As Shelby worked, her mind was consumed with thoughts of the latest clues in their quest to find the mysterious artifact. The ghostly words of Prudence Harris, spoken from her portrait at the Harris Estate, still echoed in her mind, a haunting reminder of the challenge that lay ahead.

"It's been days since we were at the Harris Estate," Shelby said, her face looking pensive. "Thanks to Emily, our resident ghost, we found the tunnel Prudence mentioned, but we're no closer to understanding where to look for the stones that were used for something useful. I think it could be a stonewall, but how on earth will we find the right one?"

Harper, perched atop a nearby shelf, tilted her head thoughtfully. "We don't know for sure it is a stonewall we're looking for," she mused, her tail swishing back and forth. "Maybe it's something made from stones."

Shelby paused, a stack of books in her arms, and considered the cat's words. "Like what?" she asked, her eyes narrowed in concentration.

"A house, an old foundation?" Harper offered, her clever eyes glinting in the lamplight.

Shelby sighed, the weight of their quest heavy on her shoulders. "I just don't know," she admitted, carefully placing the books on their new shelf. "We need help."

As they pondered their next move, Harper suddenly grew still, her gaze fixed intently on the checkout counter across the room. Shelby followed the cat's line of sight, her eyes widening as she noticed a faint glimmering in the air, like a scattering of tiny, luminous particles.

Myths and Magic

"Harper, what do you see?" Shelby asked, her voice barely above a whisper. "Is Emily here?"

The cat blinked slowly, her eyes distant and unfocused. After a moment, she turned to Shelby. "Emily said we should go to the small park where the tunnel ends."

Shelby's heart skipped a beat, a flutter of excitement mixed in her chest. "Why? What's there?"

Harper shook her head, her whiskers twitching with uncertainty. "That's all she told me. It takes a lot of energy for Emily to communicate with me. She can't tell me much before she becomes exhausted and disappears."

Shelby glanced at the clock on the wall, its hands pointing well past the witching hour. "When are we supposed to go to the park?"

"Now," Harper informed her, leaping down from the shelf with a soft thud.

Without hesitation, Shelby and Harper made their way out of the bookshop, the cool night air washing over them as they stepped into the quiet streets of Hamlet. The town was bathed in the soft, silvery glow of the moonlight, the shadows long and deep as they made their way toward the park.

As they walked, Shelby had that awful feeling

they were being watched, that some unseen presence was tracking them. She glanced over her shoulder, her eyes scanning the streets for any sign of movement, but the town was still and silent, the only sound the soft echo of their footsteps on the pavement.

Harper, sensing Shelby's unease, pressed closer to the young woman, offering a comforting presence in the darkness. "It's okay," the cat murmured, her voice soft and reassuring. "I don't sense anything."

Shelby nodded, drawing strength from her companion's support. "Why do you think Emily wants us to go to the park?"

"I can't even venture a guess," the cat told her.

As they entered the park and followed the neatly laid out paths, the silence was almost eerie. The only sound was the soft rustling of leaves in the gentle breeze. Shelby and Harper moved cautiously, their senses heightened and alert, scanning the darkness for any sign of movement or danger.

Suddenly, a voice spoke from behind them, shattering the stillness of the night. "Hello, Shelby. You're out late. It's nearly 2 am."

Shelby and Harper whirled around, their hearts pounding hard, to find Evelyn Blackwell standing just feet away. The woman was dressed casually in jeans, a light pullover sweater, and a baseball cap, her dark eyes glinting with an expression Shelby couldn't quite put her finger on.

Shelby swallowed hard, trying to keep her voice steady as she replied, "So are you."

Evelyn smiled, a slight curve of her lips that didn't quite reach her eyes. "I like walking around at night when I can't sleep. It's peaceful and quiet." She paused, her gaze drifting to the shadows behind Shelby. "Did you happen to locate the book I was looking for?"

"No," Shelby almost shouted, her nerves frayed and on edge.

Evelyn studied her for a moment, her head tilted slightly to the side. "Perhaps," she mused, her voice soft and cryptic, "the book is more useful to someone else."

Shelby's mind raced, trying to make sense of the woman's words. What did she know about the book? And what did she mean by it being more useful to someone else?

As if sensing Shelby's unease, Evelyn's gaze sharpened, her eyes narrowing slightly. "Are you looking for someone?" she asked, her voice low and probing. "Is that why you're out so late?"

Shelby shook her head, her heart hammering in her chest. "No, we're just out for a walk. I couldn't sleep," she fibbed. "I needed to clear my head."

Evelyn's hand moved toward the pocket of her sweater, and Shelby's eyes widened in alarm. She took a quick step back, her mind racing with the possibility that the woman might be reaching for a weapon, but as Evelyn's hand emerged, Shelby saw that it was only her phone, and she felt a flush of embarrassment at her overreaction.

Evelyn noticed Shelby's sudden movement, and a flicker of something – amusement, perhaps, or understanding – crossed her face. "It seems you have things to worry about," she said, her voice low and cryptic. "I must be going."

As she turned to walk away, she paused, glancing back over her shoulder at the young woman and the cat. "Be careful, you two."

Shelby and Harper watched as Evelyn disappeared into the night, her form melting into the shadows as if she had never been there at all. For a long moment, they stood in silence, their minds reeling from the strange encounter.

"How did she sneak up on us like that?" Shelby whispered, her voice trembling slightly.

Harper, her fur standing on end, shook her head. "No idea."

Myths and Magic

Shelby's mind whirled, trying to make sense of Evelyn's words and actions. "Was she watching and trailing us?"

"Again, no idea," Harper replied, her eyes still fixed on the spot where Evelyn had vanished. "But there's something about her, something that doesn't quite add up."

Shelby nodded, a shiver running down her spine despite the warmth of the night. "Is she trying to trick us? Is she trying to get us to drop our guard? Is she trying to convince us she doesn't have evil intentions about the magical book?"

"We need to give this some thought," Harper responded.

"What did Evelyn mean that maybe the book is more useful to someone else?" Shelby wondered aloud, pushing a strand of hair from her eyes. "And what did she mean that I have things to be worried about?"

Harper turned toward home, her tail held high and her steps purposeful. "Maybe exactly what she said," the cat mused, her voice low and thoughtful. "You do have things to worry about. That might be the reason Emily sent us here. To figure out if someone is friend or foe."

"How do we know who we can trust?" Shelby groaned.

As they made their way around the park, Harper's eyes scanned the shadows, searching for anything that might provide a clue or a hint as to their next move, but the night was still and silent. The only sound was the soft padding of their footsteps on the grass.

"Come on," Harper said at last, her voice firm and determined. "Let's go home. We have a lot to think about, and we need to be ready for whatever comes next."

As they walked, Shelby's mind churned with the events of the night, trying to piece together the puzzle of Evelyn's cryptic words and the ghostly message from Emily. She knew they were getting close to the answers that were just beyond their grasp, but she also knew they couldn't drop their guard since the dark forces that sought to claim the artifact for their own would stop at nothing to see their twisted dreams realized.

As they stepped into the warm, welcoming glow of the bookshop, Shelby felt a sense of safety. Shelby felt strongly the encounter with Evelyn had been more than just a chance meeting. There was something about the woman's words, the way she seemed to know more than she was letting on, that set Shelby's nerves on edge.

Harper, sensing her friend's unease, leapt up onto the counter, her muscles tight with a fierce protectiveness.

"Whatever happens," the cat said, her voice low and determined, "you have me, Travis, and Lucy. We're a team."

As warmth spread through her chest at the support and love that radiated from the cat's words, Shelby was grateful for her sweet, loyal companion.

"I know," she said softly, reaching out to scratch Harper behind the ears. "I'm so thankful for all of you. I don't know what I'd do without your friendship and your courage."

She knew she had strength on her side – the love and loyalty of her friends, the wisdom of her ancestors, and the magic that flowed through her veins. As the stars twinkled in the velvet sky, Shelby was determined to unravel the clues, find the artifact, and protect the magic in the town they loved.

"Come on, Harper. Let's go upstairs and get some rest."

21

The sun was just beginning to set over the quaint town of Hamlet, and it sent a soft, pretty light through the windows of the Spellbound Bookshop. Inside, Shelby moved about the shop, her mind focused on the tasks at hand as she tidied the shelves and prepared to close up for the evening.

As she worked, Harper sat perched atop the counter, watching the young woman's every move. The cat had been by Shelby's side through thick and thin and would continue to be a source of comfort and support in the face of the challenges that lay ahead.

With a final sweep of the shop and a quick check of the locks, Shelby gathered her things and headed toward the stairs that led to her cozy apartment above. Harper leapt down from the counter and followed close behind, her tail swishing with contentment as they climbed the steps together.

Once inside, Shelby set about preparing their dinner, the aroma of spaghetti with veggie sauce and garlic bread filling the small kitchen with a mouth-watering scent. As she stirred the sauce and checked the pasta, her mind wandered to the mysterious book that had become a part of her life.

Each day, she had been examining the ancient tome, hoping against hope that the next section might have translated itself, revealing new clues and insights into the location of the artifact. But so far, the pages had remained stubbornly indecipherable, the strange symbols and foreign language taunting her with their secrets.

As they sat down to eat, the kitchen lamps cast a cozy light over the table where Shelby was lost in thought, her fork twirling absently in the strands of spaghetti. Harper, sensing her friend's distraction, nudged Shelby's hand with her nose, breaking the spell.

"Penny for your thoughts?" the cat asked the young woman with her mind, her head tilted to the side with curiosity.

Shelby sighed, setting down her fork and

running a hand through her hair. "I just can't stop thinking about the book," she admitted. "I feel like we're so close to finding the artifact, but every time I think we've made progress, we hit another dead end."

Harper nodded, her whiskers twitching with understanding. "I know it's frustrating," she said, "but we can't give up now. We've come too far to let a few setbacks stop us."

Shelby managed a small smile. "You're right," she said, her voice growing stronger with each word. "We have to keep going, no matter what. The town is counting on us ... even though most of the citizens don't know anything about it."

Feeling more positive about the situation, they finished their meals and made their way to the living room, where the book rested on the coffee table like a silent sentinel. Shelby took a deep breath and reached out, her fingers trembling slightly as she opened the cover and turned to the next section.

And then, the words began to shimmer and shift before her eyes, the ancient symbols morphing and rearranging themselves into clear, legible text. Shelby's heart raced with excitement as she read the words aloud, her voice barely above a whisper.

"These words become understandable when the

time is right," she breathed, her eyes wide with wonder. "This section of the book ... it's talking about a hiding place made of stone, where the artifact is hidden."

Harper leaned in closer, her own eyes scanning the page with focused attention. "Look," she said, her paw pointing to a line near the bottom. "It says, 'Be soft-footed. Be silent. Be safe.' What do you think that means?"

Shelby's eyes narrowed in concentration as she tried to make sense of the cryptic message. "I'm not sure," she admitted. "I think it's telling us to be careful, to tread lightly, and avoid drawing attention to ourselves."

As the implications of the book's words began to sink in, Shelby felt a flicker of fear creep into her heart, a cold, creeping dread that made her shiver despite the warmth of the room. She knew that finding the artifact was only half the battle - once they had it in their possession, they would need to act quickly and decisively to keep it safe from those who sought to use its power for their own nefarious purposes.

Harper, sensing her friend's unease, pressed close to Shelby's side, her purr a comforting rumble in the stillness of the room. "We can do this," she said, her voice filled with quiet conviction. "We've faced worse odds before and come out on top. As long as we stick together, there's nothing we can't handle."

With a deep breath and a final glance at the book, Shelby closed the cover and set it aside, her mind already racing with plans. She knew they needed to act fast, to follow the clues and unravel the mysteries that had been laid out before them.

But first, they needed to rest, to gather their strength and their wits for the tasks ahead so, as the night wore on and the stars twinkled in the velvet sky, Shelby and Harper curled up together on the couch, their hearts full of hope.

∼

As the sun dipped below the horizon, Shelby, feeling happy and relieved that the words in the book had finally been translated, bustled about her cozy apartment, preparing for the arrival of her dear friend Mr. Peacock and her acquaintance Professor Rundle.

The aroma of freshly brewed coffee and tea mingled with the savory scent of the appetizers she had carefully arranged on the kitchen table - miniature pizzas, stuffed mushrooms, and a colorful array of cut-up vegetables with a creamy dip.

Harper lounged on the windowsill, her eyes scanning the street below for any sign of their guests. The cat's tail twitched with anticipation, a reflection of the nervous energy that seemed to fill the air.

At last, a soft knock at the door announced the arrival of the two men, and Shelby hurried to greet them, a warm smile spreading across her face. Mr. Peacock, dapper as ever in his light summer jacket and bow tie, and Professor Rundle, his eyes twinkling behind his wire-rimmed glasses, stepped inside, their arms open wide for hugs and greetings.

As they gathered in the living room, pouring drinks and filling their plates with the tasty snacks, Shelby felt a sense of comfort wash over her.

Settling into the plush cushions of the sofa, Shelby turned her attention to the professor, her expression tinged with concern. "How are you feeling, Professor?" she asked, her voice soft and gentle.

The older man smiled, a hint of weariness in his eyes. "Please call me Jeffrey," he insisted, clearing his throat before continuing. "Not fully back to my old self, but much better. The doctor thought I might have suffered a mini stroke. I'm not convinced that was what happened to me."

Shelby leaned forward, her elbows resting on her knees as she studied the professor's face. "Have you remembered anything about that evening?" she pressed, eager to hear what the man recalled.

Jeffrey took a sip from his wine glass, his gaze distant as he tried to piece together the fragments of his memory. "I believe I have, but it isn't enough to satisfy the police and their investigation. They think I'm an older man who had a medical emergency, and that's it. I dare say that isn't what happened at all."

Mr. Peacock nodded, his expression grave. "Jeffrey can't recall how he got to the pub that night, but other recollections have surfaced."

Adrenaline raced through Shelby's veins as her fingers drummed absently on the arm of the chair. "What have you remembered?" she asked, her voice barely above a whisper.

Jeffrey rubbed his temple and his eyes closed as he delved into the depths of his memory. "I was working at my desk in my office at the university. I decided to take a walk because I'd been hunched over my laptop for hours. It was around 8 pm. I had a lot on my mind so I sort of wandered aimlessly."

"Did you walk into town?" Shelby prompted, her eyes wide with interest.

"I did, yes," Jeffrey confirmed, his voice growing stronger as the memories began to take shape. "I went into the coffee shop near the top of Main. It was one of the only coffee places still open. I really wanted a hot coffee despite it still being hot outside."

He paused, taking another sip of wine before continuing. "I recall speaking to a woman who came in after me. I had taken my cup to a table by the windows. The woman asked if I was Professor Rundle. I asked how she knew who I was. She mentioned that she was interested in old manuscripts and knew I worked at the university. She sat down with me, and we talked for about fifteen minutes, maybe longer. She then asked if I knew Shelby Price."

Shelby's eyes went wide, her heart skipping a beat at the mention of her name. "She did?" She gasped, her voice filled with shock and disbelief.

"Indeed, she did," Jeffrey confirmed, his expression growing troubled. "I told her you had a small, old book you wanted me to take a look at." He looked off across the room, his gaze distant and unfocused. "Suddenly, I started to feel odd. I don't know how to describe it. It was like I was outside of my body, dizzy, unmoored. Then the woman told me not to meet with Shelby Price about the manuscript. If I did, I would be in grave danger."

Shelby almost jumped out of her chair, her voice rising with each word. "She said that to you?"

"She certainly did." Jeffrey nodded, his face pale and drawn. "Sitting in that coffee shop, I was falling deeper and deeper into some sort of waking slumber, and that is the last thing I recall until I woke up in the hospital."

Shelby's mind raced, as her heart pounded. "Did you tell the police this? Did they go to the coffee shop and ask about the woman you were with?" she questioned, her voice urgent.

The professor's face fell, a look of despair washing over his features. "I told them. When they went to the coffee shop, no one who worked there remembered me being in the shop that evening."

"What about the woman? Can you describe her?" Shelby pressed, leaning forward in her seat.

With a slow shake of his head, the professor frowned. "I can't. I don't remember what she looked like. It's as if an eraser wiped out everything about her." He sat up straighter, his voice filled with quiet desperation. "It is quite disturbing. It's as if I made the whole thing up." He looked from Shelby to Mr.

Peacock and back again, his eyes asking for understanding. "I did not make this up."

Mr. Peacock, his expression thoughtful, spoke up. "I think Jeffrey was drugged by that woman," he announced, his voice firm and decisive. "She must have used some fast-acting drug. It's the only thing that makes sense."

Shelby nodded. "Did you have your briefcase with you?" she asked, turning her attention back to the professor.

"I had a backpack," he replied.

"Were the contents intact when you looked at it after you were in the hospital?" Shelby questioned. "I wonder if the woman stole from you."

"Everything was still there," Jeffrey assured her, before adding, "Although, my things seemed disturbed as if someone had rustled through them."

"I bet you were drugged so you would recall very little about the woman who threatened you." Mr. Peacock had an angry tone in his voice.

Shelby nodded, her facial features grim. "I think you're right."

As the three friends continued to discuss the strange events of that night, Harper watched from her perch on the windowsill. The evening wore on and the conversation turned to more pleasant topics, the air filled with laughter and good cheer.

When it was time for the men to leave, Shelby walked them to the door. Professor Rundle, his face softened by the warmth of the evening, turned to her with a smile.

"I had a very nice time," he said, his voice filled with a quiet sincerity. "I'm sorry I couldn't be of more help."

Shelby reached out, her hand resting gently on the man's arm. "You were a lot of help," she assured him. "I'm very sorry this happened to you, and I'm sorry if somehow I had something to do with it."

The professor shook his head. "You did not," he insisted, his voice firm and unwavering. "That woman is guilty of poisoning me. It is all on her. If I ever see her again..." He trailed off, his eyes darkening for a moment before softening once more.

"Well, I hope you never do," Shelby said, her voice filled with a protective quality.

As the two men disappeared into the night, their footsteps echoing softly on the cobblestone streets, Shelby closed the door and leaned against it, her mind twirling with all that she had learned. Harper, sensing her friend's unease, leapt down from the windowsill and wound herself around Shelby's legs, rubbing her cheeks on the young woman's leg.

"Mr. Peacock was right" the cat mewed, her voice filled with a quiet confidence. "That woman drugged Professor Rundle to keep him from remembering much about meeting her."

"If only he'd recalled what she looked like."

"Come on. It's late," the cat said. "Let's get some rest."

As Shelby drifted off to sleep, her dreams were filled with visions of being chased, of being in danger, and of almost losing her life. She woke briefly in the middle of the night and lay there looking up at the ceiling. After a few minutes, she sighed and turned over on her side, hoping that when the morning came and the sun rose over the rooftops of Hamlet, she and Harper would be ready.

22

It was dark outside Shelby's cozy apartment as she and Travis sat together, thinking about the mysterious book and the clues it held within its pages. Shelby, holding her hands tightly together in her lap, confided in Travis about her growing sense of unease and frustration.

"The final section of the book," she began, her voice tinged with a mix of apprehension, "it's only partially translated. I feel so antsy and anxious, wishing the last part would just reveal itself, transforming the symbols from that ancient language into English."

Travis, his eyes filled with understanding, reached for the book. His fingers gently turned the pages until he reached the last section. As he studied the symbols, a flicker of movement caught his eye, and he noticed a faint shimmering on the page, as if the ink itself were alive and shifting.

"Shelby, look," he said, his voice urgent as he handed the book to her. "There's something happening with the text."

The moment Shelby's fingers touched the yellowed pages, a strange sensation coursed through her, a tingling warmth that seemed to emanate from the heart of the book. Before her eyes, the symbols began to change, morphing and rearranging themselves until they formed words and phrases she could understand. Next to the words, there was a small drawing of a pine forest.

"The final clue," she breathed, her voice barely above a whisper as she read the words out loud. "'The heart of the guardian, the key to the past.' There's a drawing of a wooded area next to the words." She looked up. "But what does that mean?"

Travis, his eyes bright with a sudden realization, turned to face her, his hand reaching out to clasp hers. "You're the guardian, Shelby," he said, his voice filled with a quiet certainty. "It must mean that you're connected to the past, linked to the guardians who came before you."

Shelby stared at him. She knew she was part of

a lineage of protectors, entrusted with the duty of safeguarding the artifact, but how did that help her?

"It must mean," Travis continued, his voice growing stronger, "that you're going to succeed in protecting the artifact, just as those before you have done."

A flicker of hope ignited in Shelby's heart, a small, fragile flame that burned brightly against the darkness of her doubts and fears. Even as she clung to that hope, a nagging question tugged at the back of her mind.

"But where is it?" she asked, her voice filled with a worried tone. "We still don't know where the artifact is hidden. How are we going to find it? I feel like we're running out of time."

As if in response to her question, Harper, who had been quietly observing the conversation from her perch on the windowsill, suddenly sat up straight, her eyes wide and alert. In the corner of the room, she spotted a swirl of shining particles, dancing and shimmering in the air like tiny stars.

"Shelby," the cat mewed to the young woman's mind, her voice filled with a quiet urgency. "Emily is here. She's trying to tell us something."

With her heart racing, Shelby watched Harper's

ears twitching as the cat listened to the ghostly message.

"She says we have to go to the woods off of Pine Street," Harper relayed, her voice filled with excitement. "She says you'll know what to do when we get there."

"I think I know what to do." Shelby repeated the cat's words to Travis. "We have to go to the woods near Pine Street."

Without hesitation, the man jumped to his feet, his hand outstretched to Shelby. "Let's go," he said. "We can walk there. It's a little less than a mile. I think it will be safer than driving."

Shelby nodded, her own resolve hardening like steel as she took Travis's hand and allowed him to pull her to her feet. She quickly grabbed two flashlights from the kitchen drawer, checking to ensure the batteries were fresh. As an afterthought, she also picked up a small backpack, tossing in a bottle of water, some snacks, and a small first-aid kit. In their line of work, one could never be too prepared. Then she texted Lucy, who was out with her boyfriend, Ross, to tell her where they were going and why.

> Just in case, use the app on your phone to track me so you know where I am.

Together, with Harper leading the way, they set off from the apartment, their footsteps echoing in the stillness of the night as they made their way toward the woods. The cool evening air brushed against their skin, carrying with it the faint scent of the sea.

As they walked, the darkness seemed to press in around them, the shadows growing longer and deeper with each passing step. The air was thick with the scent of pine and earth, and the only sound was the soft rustling of leaves in the gentle breeze.

While the night closed in around them, Shelby felt the familiar feeling they were being watched, that some unseen presence was tracking their every move. She glanced all around, her eyes scanning the empty streets for any sign of someone nearby, but there was nothing, only the inky blackness of the night.

Travis, sensing her unease, reached out and took her hand, his fingers lacing with hers in a gesture of comfort and support. "It's okay," he murmured, his voice low and reassuring. "We're together."

Shelby nodded, drawing strength from his presence, the warmth of his touch, and the steadiness of his gaze.

"I'm so sorry I dragged you into this," Shelby told him.

"You didn't drag me into anything. I came willingly." A little smile played over the man's lips. "Besides, *you're* the one who got dragged into all this. You didn't ask for it."

"But it's too dangerous. I should have handled it on my own."

Travis stopped walking and turned to her. "No, you shouldn't have. You were pulled into this whole thing, and you accepted the challenge. We have a connection between us, Shelby. We help each other; we support each other. If something bad happens, it isn't your fault." He gently ran his finger down Shelby's cheek. "I'm here by choice, and you're doing what you have to do."

Harper trilled softly at the man's words, and Shelby closed her eyes and gave a slight nod.

"Come on," Travis said. "Let's go see what we're supposed to find."

As they neared the woods, the trees looming tall and dark against the starlit sky, Shelby felt a sense of foreboding, a prickling at the back of her neck that warned of some unseen danger lurking just beyond the shadows.

Harper, her fur standing on end and her tail puffed up in alarm, pressed close to Shelby's side, her eyes scanning the darkness for any sign of threat. "Something's not right," the cat mewed, her voice barely audible over the pounding of Shelby's heart. "We need to be careful."

Shelby and Travis exchanged a glance, their expressions grim and determined as they stepped into the woods, the branches reaching out to snag at their clothing like grasping fingers. The air grew cooler as they made their way deeper into the forest, the moonlight filtering through the leaves in eerie, dappled patterns on the forest floor.

The beam of Shelby's flashlight cut through the darkness, casting long shadows that seemed to dance and flicker with a life of their own. The sound of their footsteps was muffled by the soft carpet of leaves and moss underfoot, and the only other noise was the occasional hoot of an owl or the distant rustling of some unseen creature in the undergrowth.

After what felt like an eternity, they finally emerged into a small clearing, where an ancient stone wall weaved around the perimeter of an old cemetery like a silent sentinel. Shelby's breath caught in her throat as she realized where they were standing - the old graveyard, where generations of Hamlet's residents lay buried beneath the earth.

At the center of the clearing, stood a weathered mausoleum, its crumbling walls and moss-covered roof speaking of centuries of neglect and decay. Shelby's heart raced as she approached the structure, her eyes scanning the faded inscriptions and crumbling stonework for any sign of the clue they sought.

And then, as if in answer to her unspoken question, the words of the final clue echoed in her mind once more. "The heart of the guardian, the key to the past."

With trembling fingers, Shelby reached up and grasped the pink quartz pendant that hung around her neck, the stone warm and heavy against her skin. Could it be? Could this simple piece of jewelry, passed down through generations of her family, be the key to unlocking the secrets of the past?

Taking a deep breath, Shelby stepped forward, her hand outstretched as she pressed the pendant against the cold, unyielding stone of the mausoleum's door. For a moment, nothing happened, and a flicker of doubt crept into her heart.

But then, as if in response to some ancient, unspoken command, the pendant began to glow, a soft, pulsing light that seemed to come from the heart of the stone. Shelby watched in awe as the light grew brighter and brighter until it was almost blinding in its intensity.

With a soft click and a grating of stone against stone, the door to the mausoleum slowly swung open, revealing a dark, yawning passageway that promised to hold the answers they had been seeking for so many weeks.

"Amazing," Travis whispered in awe.

He, Shelby, and Harper stood at the threshold, their hearts beating with trepidation as they peered into the darkness beyond.

Travis placed a reassuring hand on Shelby's shoulder, his touch a comforting presence in the face of the unknown. "We've got this," he said, his voice filled with quiet confidence. "It'll be okay."

Harper, her tail held high and her eyes gleaming with determination, stepped forward, ready to lead the way into the depths of the mausoleum.

"Emily brought us here for a reason," she mewed to Shelby, her voice filled with a quiet certainty. "We have to trust in the magic that guides us and in the strength of our own hearts."

"Wait," Shelby told them. "I want to do a protection spell to help keep us safe." Using her training, the young woman closed her eyes, touched her pendant, and said the words aloud. "Sacred guardians of light and might, I call upon you on this night. Wrap us in your loving embrace, shield us from harm, and keep us safe.

"From darkness and danger, protect our way. Let the negative fade and the positive stay. With this spell, I set the seal, keep us safe, this is my appeal.

"By earth, fire, air, and sea, I pray that you will let it be."

When the spell was cast, Harper trilled.

"Okay, let's go." Shelby took a deep breath as she stepped forward, ready to unravel the mystery of the artifact, once and for all. The guardian and her companions disappeared into the darkness, their footsteps echoing in the stillness of the night as they ventured inside to face the unknown.

23

Inside the crumbling walls of the old mausoleum, Shelby felt a palpable sense of anticipation, a tingling in her bones that told her the artifact was near. The air was thick with the musty scent of age and decay, and the only sound was the soft whisper of their breath and the pounding of their hearts.

Travis and Harper stood to the side, their eyes fixed on Shelby as she moved to the center of the cool, damp chamber. The beam of her flashlight danced over the weathered stone, casting eerie shadows that seemed to flicker and dance with a life of their own.

Again, Shelby closed her eyes and took a deep, steadying breath as she reached out with her mind, trying to sense the artifact's presence. At first, there was nothing, just the cold, empty darkness that pressed in around her, but then, slowly, a warmth began to build, a gentle heat that seemed to come from the far wall of the mausoleum.

Her palms sweaty, Shelby stepped forward. Her hand reached out and her fingers ran over the rough, pitted surface of the stones. As she moved closer to the corner, the heat intensified, growing almost unbearable until, with a gasp, she pulled her hand back, feeling as though she had been burned.

"I think it's right here," she whispered, her voice sounding shaky. "This stone ... it feels hot to the touch."

Travis moved to her side, his eyes wide with anticipation. "Where? Which one?" he asked.

Shelby pointed to a small, unremarkable stone set into the wall, its surface worn smooth by the passage of time. Travis studied it for a moment, his eyes narrowed in concentration. "Do you want me to try to remove it from the wall?"

"Maybe." Shelby stared at the stone. "Wait. I think I know what to do. "I'm going to touch it with my pendant," she said, her voice filled with a quiet certainty. "Maybe that's the key."

With shaking fingers, Shelby slipped the delicate chain from around her neck, the pink quartz pendant glinting softly in the beam of the flashlight. Taking a few deep breaths and squaring her shoulders, she pressed the stone against the wall, holding it there for a long, tense moment.

With a sudden, blinding flash of light, the stone began to rotate, grinding against the surrounding masonry with a sound like the grating of ancient bones. Slowly, it turned, revealing a small, dark opening set into the heart of the wall.

"There's a box inside," Shelby breathed, her voice so soft Travis and Harper barely heard her. With trembling hands, she reached into the opening, her fingers closing around a small, wooden container that seemed to thrum with a strange, otherworldly energy.

Carefully, reverently, she lifted the box from its hiding place, holding it before her like a sacred relic. She glanced at Travis and Harper, her eyes wide as a shiver of fear slipped over her skin. Slowly, carefully, she lifted the lid.

Inside, nestled on a bed of soft, black velvet, was a small, silver coin, its surface glowing with an inner light that seemed to pulse and flicker like a living thing. Strange symbols and characters were etched into its surface, the same mysterious language that filled the pages of the ancient book in Shelby's apartment.

"I've never seen anything like it," Travis murmured, his voice filled with awe. "Not in real life, and not in any of the history books I've studied."

He reached out, his fingers hovering just above the coin's shimmering surface, but before he could touch it, a sudden, blinding flash of light erupted from its center, forcing him to pull his hand back with a cry of shock and pain.

Harper, her ears twitching and her tail puffed up in alarm, suddenly turned toward the entrance of the mausoleum, her eyes wide with fear. "I think I heard something outside," she mewed, her voice echoing in Shelby's mind. "Footsteps, coming this way. We need to grab the coin and get out of here. Now."

Without hesitation, Shelby reached into the box, her fingers closing around the coin. To her amazement, it felt warm to the touch, almost alive, and as she lifted it from its velvet bed, she could feel a strange, tingling energy coursing through her body, filling her with a sense of power and purpose, unlike anything she had ever known.

Myths and Magic

She stared at the coin in her hand, her mind reeling with the enormity of what they had discovered. This tiny, glowing disc, no larger than a quarter, held the key to protecting the magic of Hamlet, keeping its people safe from the dark forces that sought to destroy them.

"We have to get to the tunnel," Shelby said, her voice filled with determination. "We can't let them get their hands on this."

Quickly, she slipped the coin into the pocket of her jeans, feeling its comforting weight against her leg as she turned to face her companions.

Travis, his face grim and his hand resting on the butt of his gun, nodded in agreement. "Let me go first," he said, his voice low and urgent. "I'll make sure the coast is clear."

With a final, determined glance at Shelby and Harper, the detective stepped out into the night, his eyes scanning the shadows for any sign of danger. The air was cold and still, the only sound the soft rustling of leaves in the breeze and the distant hooting of an owl.

"It looks clear," he called back, his voice tense with anticipation. "We need to move fast. Follow me, and stay close."

Shelby and Harper exchanged a glance, fear

rushing through their veins as they stepped out of the mausoleum and into the eerie stillness of the cemetery. The rows of weathered gravestones stretched out before them like silent sentinels, their surfaces nearly worn smooth by the passage of time and the relentless march of the elements.

They moved quickly, hugging the tree line and sticking to the shadows as they made their way toward the road that would lead them back to town. Shelby's mind raced with what they had accomplished and the weight of the responsibility that now rested on her shoulders.

As they neared the edge of the cemetery, a sudden thought struck her, and she reached out to grab Travis's arm, pulling him to a stop.

"Maybe we should split up," she suggested, her voice urgent. "If the evil-doers are out there, they won't know which of us has the artifact. We can take different routes back to the tunnel, and throw them off our trail."

Travis frowned. "I don't like it," he said, shaking his head. "We're stronger together. If we split up, we'll be more vulnerable."

But Shelby was insistent, her eyes blazing with determination. "It's our best chance," she argued, her voice filled with a quiet intensity. "We have to do whatever it takes to protect the artifact and keep it out of their hands."

Travis hesitated for a moment, his gaze searching Shelby's face for any sign of doubt or uncertainty, but he saw only the fiery determination that burned bright in her eyes.

"All right," he said at last. "But please, be careful, Shelby."

She nodded, a small, sad smile tugging at the corners of her lips. "I will," she promised, her hand reaching out to brush his cheek. "And you be careful too, Travis. If we see the evil-doers, we'll head off in separate directions."

With a final, lingering glance, they moved on together, their footsteps echoing softly in the stillness of the night. Harper, her fur standing on end and her eyes shining with a fierce, protective light, followed close at Shelby's heels.

As they ran, weaving through the shadows and darting between the trees, Shelby's body was full of fear. She could feel the weight of the coin in her pocket, the warmth of its power seeping into her skin.

Even as the thrill of their discovery coursed

through her veins, she felt certain that they were being watched, that someone was tracking their every move. The hairs on the back of her neck stood on end, and a shiver of unease ran down her spine, a primal warning of dangers ahead.

Just as they reached the edge of the park, a sudden, chilling voice rang out from the shadows, stopping Shelby dead in her tracks.

"Hello, Shelby."

She whirled around, her heart leaping into her throat as she saw the familiar figure of Evelyn Blackwell stepping out from behind a tree, her face twisted into a cruel, mocking smile. The man who had attempted to steal a book from Shelby's shop stood right behind the woman.

"Evelyn," Shelby breathed, her voice trembling with anger. "All this time, I thought it might be you. You're one of them."

Evelyn laughed, a cold, mirthless sound that sent shivers down Shelby's spine. "Foolish girl," she sneered, her eyes filled with a malevolent light. "You have no idea of the powers you're dealing with, but it doesn't matter now. The artifact will be mine, and there's nothing you can do to stop me."

Shelby's hand closed around the coin in her pocket, her fingers tightening with a fierce, protective grip. She glanced at Harper, her eyes blazing with a silent plea for help, for the strength and courage to face the evil that stood before them.

With a sudden, savage cry, Harper leapt forward, her claws extended and her teeth bared in a snarl of rage. She slashed at Evelyn's face, her fur standing on end as she fought with all the strength and fury of a mother defending her young.

Evelyn screamed, her hands flying to her bloodied cheek as she staggered back, her eyes wide with shock and pain as the man she was with tried to help her. Then, in that moment, Shelby and Travis saw their chance, their one opportunity to escape and make their way back to the safety of the tunnel.

"Run!" Shelby shouted to him, her voice ringing out like a clarion call in the stillness of the night. "Don't let them get it, Travis!"

And with that, they split up heading in different directions, their feet pounding against the hard-packed earth as they raced through the darkness, their hearts filled with a desperate, unyielding hope they could outrun the evil that pursued them, find a way to keep the artifact safe, and protect the magic of Hamlet.

As Shelby and Travis raced through the night with desperate urgency, the sound of pursuit echoed behind each of them. The man who had been with Evelyn, his face twisted into a snarl of rage and determination, started after the detective, his footsteps heavy and pounding against the earth.

Shelby, her shoes smacking the pavement as she ran, headed for town by a different road, her mind racing with a frantic need to reach the safety of the tunnel. In moments, she could hear Evelyn's footsteps coming after her, the sound of the woman's labored breathing filling the air.

With Harper beside her, Shelby weaved through the side roads of Hamlet, darting into shadows and ducking behind trees as she tried to shake her pursuer. They ran and hid, their movements quick and furtive, as they attempted to reach the small park where the tunnel entrance lay hidden.

As she rounded the last street and entered the park, her lungs burning with the effort of her flight, Shelby could hear Evelyn's feet, the sound growing closer with every passing second, but then, out of the corner of her eye, she spotted a familiar figure standing under the trees.

"Shelby!" Lucy called out, her voice ringing through the stillness of the night as she took off at a sprint, heading straight for her friend. "I'll stop her. Keep going!"

With a fierce cry, Lucy raced toward Evelyn, her eyes blazing. She charged at the woman with all her strength, slamming into her with the full force of her body. Evelyn stumbled and fell, her arms flailing as she tried to keep her balance, and Lucy went down with her, the two of them tumbling to the ground in a tangle of limbs.

They fought each other on the grass, rolling and grappling as they traded blows and kicks. Lucy's face was a mask of grim determination as she tried to keep Evelyn pinned down to buy Shelby and Harper the time they needed to reach the tunnel and hide the artifact.

Shelby raced into the tunnel, her veins filled with a sickening dread as she and Harper hurried to the spot in the wall where they had prepared the hiding place for the artifact. But as they drew closer, they saw something that made them both come to a sudden, horrified halt.

The man who had been with Evelyn had Travis in a chokehold, his arm wrapped tight around the detective's neck as he struggled to break free. Travis's face was pale and strained, his eyes wide with fear and anger.

"Run, Shelby," he shouted, his voice hoarse and

choked with the pressure of the man's grip. "Get out of here, now!"

But Shelby and Harper didn't run. Instead, they slowly walked forward, their eyes locked on the man and their faces twisted into identical expressions of rage and determination.

"You didn't give this thug the artifact, did you?" Shelby asked, her voice dripping with false bravado as she pretended that Travis had been carrying the magical coin.

Before leaving Shelby's apartment, Travis had placed a shiny rock in his pocket, a decoy in case he was caught, so that he could pretend he was the one carrying the artifact. And now, as he struggled against the man's grip, he saw the glimmer of understanding in Shelby's eyes.

"He thinks you have it," Travis gasped out, his voice strained with the effort of speaking.

Shelby forced herself to paste a sickening grin on her face, her eyes never leaving the man's face as she spoke. "You think you know everything," she said to Travis's assailant, her voice low and mocking.

And then, to the shock and amazement of everyone in the tunnel, Harper spoke, her voice ringing out clear and strong. "But you don't know anything," she said to the man, her eyes flashing with a fierce, unyielding light.

The man stared at the cat in disbelief, his grip on Travis loosening for just a fraction of a second, and in that moment, Shelby saw her chance.

"Now!" she screamed, her voice echoing off the walls of the tunnel.

Harper flung herself at the man, her claws extended and her teeth bared in a snarl of fury. At the same time, Shelby ran forward, her leg swinging out in a powerful kick that caught the man square in the kneecap.

He howled in pain, his grip on Travis slipping as he staggered back. Travis wrenched himself free, whirling around to face his attacker with fierce determination.

He wrestled the man to the ground, his fists flying as he pummeled him with all the strength he could muster, and then, with a final, decisive blow, he brought the butt of his gun down on the man's head, knocking him out cold.

For a moment, the tunnel was silent, the only sound the harsh panting of their breath.

Shelby spoke. "Quick," she said, her eyes wide with urgency. "We have to get the artifact into its hiding spot before anyone else comes in here."

Travis nodded, his face serious as he hurried to the place in the wall where they had prepared the hiding spot. With quick, efficient movements, he removed the heavy rock that concealed the opening and yanked out the box he had prepared for the artifact.

Shelby reached into her pocket, her fingers shaking as she grabbed the magical coin from its hiding place. It was no longer hot to the touch so she handed it to Travis, watching as he placed it carefully in the box, his hands steady and sure.

He pushed the box back into the hole, moving the dirt and rocks around it to conceal its presence, and then, as he worked to fill in the opening, Shelby's eyes widened with a sudden realization.

"I hear sirens," she said, her voice trembling with exhaustion. "Lucy is still out there, in the park. She tried to stop Evelyn from chasing me."

Harper, her ears twitching with urgency, turned toward the entrance of the tunnel. "Finish filling in the hole," she told them, her voice low and commanding. "I'll go see what's happening."

And with that, the cat turned and raced away, her paws flying over the ground as she disappeared into the darkness of the tunnel.

Travis and Shelby worked quickly, their hands

Myths and Magic

moving in a desperate blur as they filled the area around the box with dirt and rocks, concealing any trace of its presence. And then, with a final, heaving effort, Travis lifted the heavy rock back into place, sealing the opening.

Shelby closed her eyes and, in her mind, recited a spell to keep the artifact hidden and protected.

"It's done," she said, her breathing fast and shallow as she leaned back against the wall of the tunnel. She turned to Travis, her eyes shining with gratitude and relief. "Thank you for your help. I couldn't have done it without you."

Exhausted, she leaned forward, resting her head on Travis's shoulder for a long, quiet moment, and then, slowly, she lifted her head, looking up into his eyes with a soft, tender expression.

Travis felt his heart fill with a sudden, overwhelming heat and a rush of emotion. Slowly, gently, he reached out, his thumb brushing over the soft skin of Shelby's cheek.

"Our memories will be wiped clean soon," he said, his voice low and rough with emotion, "and neither of us will remember this moment."

Then, without another word, he leaned down, placing his lips on Shelby's in a long, sweet kiss that seemed to stretch on forever. In that moment, everything else faded away - the danger, the fear, the uncertainty of what lay ahead. All that mattered was the feel of her in his arms, the taste of her on his lips, the knowledge that, for one brief, lovely moment, they had found each other in the darkness.

As suddenly as it had begun, the moment was over, and their memories were altered by the magic of the artifact.

Shelby and Lucy found themselves standing side by side in the park, blinking in confusion as they tried to make sense of their surroundings.

Travis was there, too, talking to a police officer who stood over the unconscious body of Evelyn's accomplice. He made eye contact with Shelby and smiled at her.

Evelyn herself stood nearby, covered in dirt and bits of grass, her face a mask of confusion and disbelief.

"I'm not sure what happened," she told the officer, her voice trembling. "I guess he and I had a fight, but I can't remember why we were even here in the park."

"Have you been drinking, ma'am?" the officer questioned.

It was clear, in that moment, that Shelby, Lucy, and Travis were not the only ones who'd had their memories wiped clean. Whatever magic had been at work, whatever power had been unleashed, it had touched them all, leaving them with nothing but a vague sense of unease.

But as Shelby looked down at Harper, who sat at her feet with a knowing glint in her eye, she had a strange feeling that everything had happened just as it was meant to.

24

The sun dipped low on the horizon as Shelby made her way back to her cozy apartment above the Spellbound Bookshop. The streets of Hamlet were busy with tourists and locals, but she could still hear the soft chirping of birds and the gentle rustling of leaves in the warm evening breeze.

As she climbed the stairs and went into her apartment, Shelby had the feeling that something was missing, a strange, unsettling sensation that tugged at the edges of her mind. She glanced around the familiar space, her eyes roaming over the bookshelves and the comfortable furniture, but nothing seemed out of place.

The magical book had disappeared, and Shelby's memory of it had been washed clean. Although she didn't understand what was missing, she still felt a sensation of loss. The artifact was now safely hidden away and was strong once again because it had been energized by Shelby when she touched it.

The artifact would continue to enhance and strengthen the magical abilities of the Paranormals in town ... until its power begins to wane again in about 100 years, and then another guardian will need to infuse it with new energy and protect it from those who wish to yield its power for evil.

There were some other things that Shelby would never know or recall. One was that it was Evelyn Blackwell who spoke with Professor Rundle in the coffee shop, threatened him not to meet with Shelby about the old book, and drugged him so he wouldn't recall details of their meeting.

Another was that Lucy had hurried to the park near the tunnel that night because she'd tracked Shelby with her phone app and saw she was heading to the tunnel. Thinking she might need help, Lucy took off and waited for Shelby at the park, then attacked Evelyn Blackwell to keep her away from her friend.

Harper, curled up on the windowsill, watched as Shelby moved about the room, her brow furrowed in confusion. The cat knew the reason for her friend's unease, the secrets that had been wiped from her memory, but she also knew that it was not her place to reveal the truth to the young woman.

A knock at the door startled Shelby from her thoughts, and she hurried to answer it. Lucy was standing on the other side, a bright smile on her face.

"Hey, you," Lucy said, stepping inside and giving Shelby a warm hug. "I thought we could grab some dinner."

"Great idea." Shelby nodded, picking up her purse and keys as they headed out into the evening. As they walked, they talked and laughed, their conversation flowing as easily as it always did. But when the topic turned to the events of the previous night, both women found themselves at a loss.

"It's the strangest thing." Lucy's eyes narrowed. "I remember being in the park with you, and I remember seeing Travis there, but I can't for the life of me remember why we were there or what we were doing."

Shelby shrugged, a flicker of unease passing over her face. "I know what you mean. I know we were out late and were so engrossed in conversation that we weren't paying attention to where we were going. How we got to the park is like a big, blank spot in my memory, and no matter how hard I try, I can't fill it in."

They lapsed into silence for a moment, each lost in their own thoughts as they tried to make sense of the gaps in their recollections, but as the evening wore on and the conversation turned to other things, the strange, unsettling feeling began to fade, replaced by the warm glow of friendship.

Later that night after she'd returned from dinner with Lucy, Shelby sat curled up on her couch when a soft knock at the door announced Travis's arrival. She felt a flutter of excitement in her chest as she opened the door, her eyes drinking in the sight of him standing there, his dark hair tousled and his eyes shining with warmth.

"Hey, you," he said, his voice low and soft as he stepped inside, his arms coming up to wrap her in a gentle hug. "I've been looking forward to this all day."

A small smile played at the corners of Shelby's mouth. "Me, too. I'm glad you're here."

They settled onto the couch, Travis's arm draped casually over Shelby's shoulders as they talked about their days. Travis told her about the case he'd been working on, the long hours and the endless dead ends, and the sense of satisfaction he'd felt when he'd finally cracked it.

"It's a good feeling," he said, his eyes distant as he remembered the moment of triumph. "Knowing that you've made a difference, that you've helped someone who needed it."

Shelby nodded, her own eyes shining with understanding. She knew that feeling well, the sense of purpose that came from using your gifts to make the world a little bit better.

As the evening wore on and the stars began to twinkle in the velvet sky, Travis and Shelby decided to head out to the small, second-floor porch, where the warm night air enveloped them like a soft blanket.

They sat at the bistro table together sipping from cool glasses of lemonade and watching the people passing by on the street below. A few minutes later, out of the corner of her eye, Shelby caught sight of a woman with dark hair and a confident stride.

"Hey," she said, nudging Travis with her elbow. "Doesn't that woman look like the one from the park last night?"

Travis squinted, his eyes following the woman as she walked arm in arm with a tall, broad-shouldered man. "Yeah, she does, but she's taller than the woman we saw. That was a strange night, wasn't it? The woman and the man she was with didn't seem to recall how they got there or why they'd had a fight. They must have been really drunk."

Shelby nodded, her mind drifting back to the events of the evening, the confusion and the uncertainty that had seemed to hang over everything like a thick, impenetrable fog.

"You're right," she said, her voice soft and distant. "That woman and the man she was with seemed really confused like they had no idea how they'd gotten there or what had happened."

Travis chuckled, shaking his head in bemusement. "I was so wrapped up in my case that night, I needed to get out and walk to clear my head. I didn't even remember walking to the park. It's like my mind just went blank, and the next thing I knew, I was standing there with the two officers."

Shelby sighed, leaning back against the back of her chair and staring up at the star-studded sky. "Really? Lucy and I were wandering around at night and were so engrossed in our conversation that we didn't even pay attention to where we were heading. We ended up in the park," she murmured, her voice barely above a whisper. "I was surprised to see you there."

"Definitely a weird night," Travis agreed.

Harper, curled up at their feet, let out a soft, knowing purr. She understood their confusion, their sense of unease, but she also knew that it was better this way. She felt badly that the couple remembered nothing of the artifact, but knew it wasn't her place to change what had happened to their memories.

As the night wore on and the conversation turned to other things, Shelby found herself increasingly aware of Travis's presence beside her, the warmth of his body, and the gentle touch of his hand on her arm.

She glanced over at him, her heart skipping a beat as she met his gaze, the electricity that had always sparked between them suddenly flaring to life. She held Travis's gaze and they both felt red hot sparks jumping between them. Shelby looked at his lips for a quick moment, and a sudden warmth rushed through her.

Travis almost reached up to brush a strand of hair from her cheek, but caught himself because he knew if he touched her at that moment, he would certainly kiss her.

For a second, something almost made him feel like they had kissed before, but he knew that was nonsense. They'd both agreed to take their relationship slow to spend time as friends before taking things any further. Still ... maybe it had happened in a dream.

Shelby's breath caught in her throat, her pulse racing as she waited for him to make a move, but with a slight sigh, Travis reached for his glass and took a long swallow from it, breaking the spell that had sparkled between them for several seconds.

She felt a flicker of disappointment, a sense of lost opportunity that tugged at her heart, but she also knew that it was for the best. They had agreed to build a foundation of friendship before rushing into anything more.

With a soft sigh, Shelby rose to her feet, stretching her arms above her head as she turned toward the door. "Shall we go in and start the movie?" she asked, her voice light and casual, betraying none of the tumult that swirled inside her.

Travis smiled. "Yeah, let's." When he stood, he reached for Shelby's hand, and they started for the door to the apartment together.

"Thanks," Shelby whispered as they were about to go in.

"For what?"

With a little chuckle, Shelby said, "I don't even know for what. I just felt like I had to say it."

"Well, whatever the reason, you're most welcome."

She paused and looked into his eyes as those glittering sparks leapt between them again. "I'm glad you're here." She squeezed his hand.

Travis smiled his beautiful smile down on her. "So am I, Shelby Price, so am I."

I hope you enjoyed *Myths and Magic*! The next book in the series, *Poison and Potions*, can be found here:

https://mybook.to/PoisonandPotions

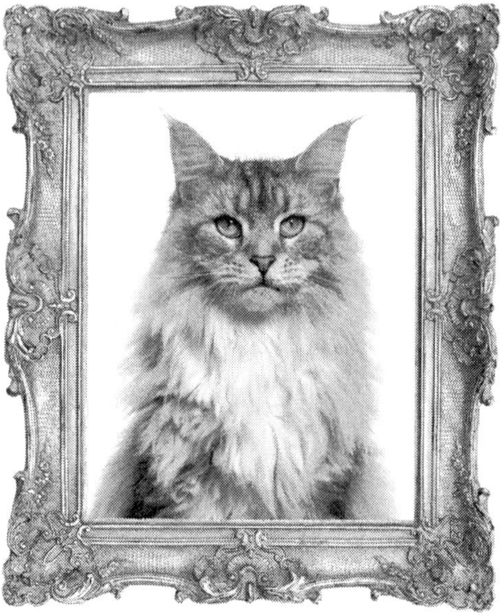

THANK YOU FOR READING!

Books by J.A. WHITING can be found here:
amazon.com/author/jawhiting

To hear about new books and book sales, please sign up for my mailing list at:
jawhiting.com

Your email will never be sold, shared, or spammed.

If you enjoyed the book, please consider leaving a review. A few words are all that's needed. It would be very much appreciated.

BOOKS BY J. A. WHITING

SPELLBOUND BOOKSHOP PARANORMAL COZY MYSTERIES

SWEET COVE PARANORMAL COZY MYSTERIES

LIN COFFIN PARANORMAL COZY MYSTERIES

CLAIRE ROLLINS PARANORMAL COZY MYSTERIES

MURDER POSSE PARANORMAL COZY MYSTERIES

PAXTON PARK PARANORMAL COZY MYSTERIES

ELLA DANIELS WITCH COZY MYSTERIES

SEEING COLORS PARANORMAL COZY MYSTERIES

OLIVIA MILLER MYSTERIES (not cozy)

SWEET ROMANCES by JENA WINTER

COZY BOX SETS

BOOKS BY J.A. WHITING & NELL MCCARTHY

HOPE HERRING PARANORMAL COZY MYSTERIES

TIPPERARY CARRIAGE COMPANY COZY MYSTERIES

BOOKS BY J.A. WHITING & ARIEL SLICK

GOOD HARBOR WITCHES PARANORMAL COZY MYSTERIES

BOOKS BY J.A. WHITING & AMANDA DIAMOND

PEACHTREE POINT COZY MYSTERIES

DIGGING UP SECRETS PARANORMAL COZY MYSTERIES

BOOKS BY J.A. WHITING & MAY STENMARK

MAGICAL SLEUTH PARANORMAL WOMEN'S FICTION COZY MYSTERIES

HALF MOON PARANORMAL MYSTERIES

VISIT US

jawhiting.com

bookbub.com/authors/j-a-whiting

amazon.com/author/jawhiting

facebook.com/jawhitingauthor

bingebooks.com/author/ja-whiting

Made in the USA
Las Vegas, NV
05 July 2024